THE HORCH AND THE
ROTTERDAM INGOTS

THE HORCH AND THE ROTTERDAM INGOTS

R.W. Strachan

Book Guild Publishing

First published in Great Britain in 2013 by
The Book Guild Ltd
9 Priory Business Park
Wistow Road, Kibworth
Leics, LE8 0RX
Copyright © R.W. Strachan 2013
Paperback edition 2016

Typesetting in Baskerville by
Keyboard Services, Luton, Bedfordshire

Printed and bound in Great Britain by
CPI Group (UK) Ltd, Croydon, CR0 4YY

A catalogue record for this book is available from
The British Library

ISBN 978 1 91087 851 4

Part 1

1

Rotterdam, Holland, May 1940

The Horch staff car stopped in front of the largest bank in Rotterdam. Four senior Wehrmacht officers alighted from the vehicle and entered the bank. Two army Opel lorries were also parked outside the bank and the NCO in charge was told to remain outside until called. Major-General Albert Backhaus entered the bank manager's office along with Colonels Grunzig and Gertsch. The major-general's staff officer, Major Otto Fromm, was also present. Major-General Backhaus informed the banker that he had been instructed by Berlin to seize the Dutch Government's gold ingots from the vault in this particular bank. The banker got up and was followed down two flights of stairs by the officers. The vault was opened and there the officers saw a pile of gold ingots.

Major-General Backhaus realised that to remove the gold back up the stairs was going to take an eternity and asked the banker if there was an easier way. The banker told him that it was not necessary to take the gold out the way they had come in and that it could be removed at the rear of the bank next to the building's car park.

The two Opel lorries were moved accordingly and the gold was loaded on to them by the soldiers. This operation took the best part of a day and many journeys were made from the bank to the army barracks, which the major-general and his men occupied. There were four thousand and forty ingots in total. However, Major-General Backhaus gave the banker a receipt for four thousand. Over the coming days the four officers removed forty ingots, which they would share once the war was over.

Colonel Grunzig had a cousin who was married to a banker in the town of Biel in Switzerland and arrangements were made for the forty ingots to be deposited there. Three trips using different motor cars were made and on each occasion ten ingots were deposited in large safety deposit boxes. However, on the final trip to Switzerland, Major Otto Fromm, who was driving the car, reached Weil am Rhein and saw that the Swiss were stopping and searching every vehicle entering from the German side. He did not cross into Switzerland and made his way back to Rotterdam. A meeting was held the following day between the cabal of four officers and they discussed the remaining ten ingots. Major Fromm suggested concealing them in the chassis legs of the Horch staff car and after a short time this was agreed. Major Fromm found a mechanic on the outskirts of Rotterdam who cut off the rear ends of the Horch's chassis legs. The following day Major Fromm returned to the mechanic's garage and had the ends restored. The mechanic was unaware of the illicit cargo but he was well paid for his work.

The four army officers remained in Holland until June 1942. When all four were sent to Russia, Colonels Grunzig and Gertsch were transferred to the 6th Army and ended up in Stalingrad where they both perished. Major-General Backhaus and his staff officer wound up in Rostov in the Don region of Russia.

2

The large German army base on the outskirts of Rostov housed some twenty-five thousand Wehrmacht soldiers. The base was part of the 4th Panzer Army, which consisted of one hundred and twenty Panther tanks and several hundred troop-carrying lorries and other vehicles including fuel tankers. The camp was the size of a large town with hundreds of Nissen huts and other prefabricated buildings, which were used to billet the troops. This unit of the 4th Panzer Army had been based at this camp since July 1942 and was awaiting instructions to seize the Soviet Union's oilfields in Azerbaijan. The order never came because the 6th Army under the command of General Paulus had become bogged down at Stalingrad and, until victory had been assured, it would have been too dangerous to move south. The officer in overall command of the Rostov base was Major-General Albert Backhaus, a veteran of the First World War. He had been living in a requisitioned dacha some two miles west of the base.

Corporal Helmut Klein was a cryptographer attached to the 4th Panzer Army and was also based at Rostov. He had been conscripted into the German Wehrmacht in 1936 and after basic training had been sent to the Wehrmacht's school of cryptography where he was trained to operate the Enigma cipher machine. He could encode and decode messages at speed.

Just after 2 p.m. on Sunday 31 January, 1943, Corporal

Klein was sitting in front of his Enigma machine when it came to life. He wrote down the message on the official pad and then, using a code book, decoded the message. He read it through twice to make sure that he had not made any errors. He rubbed his brow. He got up from his machine and donned his army greatcoat and gloves and then put on a balaclava to protect his ears. He finally placed his forage cap on top of that as the temperature outside was minus twenty degrees centigrade.

He opened the small door of the Nissen hut and walked out on to the hard packed snow. His breath started to freeze on his collar due to the extreme cold. He noticed hundreds of soldiers milling around the camp. Some were just taking exercise whilst others were working on vehicles.

Corporal Klein started to walk towards a bunker occupied by Captain Jurgen Muller. He set off at a brisk pace to keep warm. He had gone about eighty metres when suddenly and without warning a dozen Soviet fighter aircraft broke cloud cover and swooped downwards towards the army base, opening up with their cannon and machine-guns.

Corporal Klein had been somewhat shell-shocked with the message he had received from a fellow cryptographer at Stalingrad and by the time he realised what was happening it was too late. He started to run but he was cut down by machine-gun bullets. He was killed instantly and fell face down in the snow.

Captain Muller emerged from his bunker and saw the young cryptographer lying still on the snow-covered ground, which was now heavily bloodstained. The back of his army greatcoat was smouldering where the bullets had entered. Captain Muller ran towards his corporal and knelt beside him. He felt his carotid artery but there was no pulse. He knew the corporal was dead. Captain Muller then noticed that the dead corporal was holding a piece of paper in his gloved right hand. He removed it and saw that it had been torn from a cryptographer's pad. He was just about to read its contents when he heard aircraft engines. He raced back to his bunker for shelter and made it just in time before the MiG-3 and LaGG-3 fighter aircraft started to strafe the base on their second run. Captain Muller could clearly see the red star on their wings and fuselage. He saw that the Soviet fighters had come across the base in three waves with four aircraft in each, opening up everything they could fire. He watched the aircraft rise and disappear into the cloud. He listened for a full minute until the noise of the aircraft engines had receded.

Captain Muller emerged from his bunker and saw dozens of soldiers lying on the ground. Some were still whilst others were crying for help. Numerous lorries were on fire as were a number of Kübelwagens. The Nissen hut, which housed the Enigma machines, had been damaged but the Enigmas themselves were intact.

Soon soldiers were running around with fire extinguishers, trying to put out the fires. They were unable to use the water hoses as the pipes were frozen solid. Then the medics arrived including the forty doctors attached to this army unit of the 4th Panzers. The deceased were taken to a makeshift mortuary where two medical orderlies recorded their identities on official forms.

Captain Muller returned to his bunker and sat at his table and lit a Russian Kazbek cigarette. He was thirty-eight years of age but looked ten years older. He removed the cryptographer's paper from his pocket and read the contents. His Adam's apple rose and fell in his throat as he swallowed and his face grew paler. He read that on that day, Sunday 31 January, 1943, the Wehrmacht's 6th Army, commanded by General Paulus, had capitulated at Stalingrad.

Captain Muller whispered, 'Jesus, this is the beginning of the end.'

He got up from his table and put the message into his greatcoat pocket and left the bunker. He walked across the compound and found a Kübelwagen that was still intact. He sat behind the wheel and turned the ignition key. The engine started to turn over but very slowly and would not fire up. He beckoned to a young soldier who had been helping to extinguish vehicle fires. The soldier approached Captain Muller and was instructed to get a fully charged battery and jump leads.

After about five minutes the young soldier returned, the jump leads around his neck and holding the battery next to his chest. He lifted the rear seat of the Kübelwagen and attached the leads to the battery. He fixed the other end to the fresh battery. Captain Muller got behind the wheel and pressed the starter button. The engine began to turn over and after about three turns it fired up. Captain Muller instructed the soldier to put the good battery and the jump leads on the rear footwell.

He then drove to the base hospital and learned from the medical staff that there were eighty-seven personnel already in the makeshift mortuary and that the numbers would rise before nightfall. Over two hundred were either dead or injured. Captain Muller wrote the figures in his notebook. He returned to the centre of the camp and got hold of a sergeant and asked him about the number of vehicles that had been destroyed or rendered useless. He was informed that twenty-seven lorries and seven Kübelwagens were beyond repair as they had been destroyed by fire. He entered these figures in his notebook. He informed the sergeant that he was now going to report to the commanding officer, Major-General Backhaus. The sergeant stepped back and saluted.

Captain Muller got into the Kübelwagen and drove out of the army base over the hard packed snow. He kept his foot just touching the accelerator to prevent the vehicle from sliding, especially on corners as the conditions were treacherous. He drove on to the main road and motored for about two miles before turning off on to a single track, which led into a wooded area. The tall pines hung with glistening snow. After about a quarter of a mile he saw two pillboxes. Two sentries stepped out with their Mauser machine pistols pointing at him. He stopped and was asked to produce identification, which he handed to one of them. The sentry examined his papers under torchlight and handed them back to him. He then stepped back and saluted.

Captain Muller drove for another four hundred yards and stopped outside a large dacha, which was the home of Major-General Backhaus and other senior Wehrmacht officers. Captain Muller got out of the Kübelwagen. He thumped his gloved hands together as he could hardly feel the tips of his fingers. It was so cold.

He approached the entrance to the dacha and was stopped by two more sentries. One of the sentries said, 'Good evening, Captain. Can I please see some identification?'

Captain Muller replied, 'Certainly.' He produced his ID card and handed it to the sentry who examined it.

He handed it back and said, 'Thank you, Captain,' then stood back and saluted.

Captain Muller entered the dacha and asked for Major Fromm.

The sergeant said, 'Major Fromm will be here presently, Captain. Please have a seat and take the weight off your legs.'

Captain Muller sat down. After about a minute, the staff officer to the major-general, a Major Otto Fromm, approached Captain Muller. They had known each other for about two years.

Major Fromm said, 'Captain Muller, I understand that you have an urgent message for Major-General Backhaus.' Captain Muller nodded.

'Come with me.'

Captain Muller handed him the cryptographer's message.

Major Fromm adjusted his monocle and read the contents. He handed the message back to Captain Muller and said,

'We are finished, Muller, there's no stopping them now.' Both officers walked down a long corridor and eventually stopped outside a large oak door.

Major Fromm was about to knock when he heard Beethoven's 'Moonlight' Sonata being played on the piano. Major Fromm put his finger to his lips and winked at Captain Muller. The two officers stood for about two minutes until the playing stopped.

Major Fromm knocked on the door and heard the word 'Enter'. The two officers did as they were bid and found Major-General Backhaus sitting in front of a Russian piano. Major Fromm and Captain Muller both came to attention and saluted.

The room was full of stale cigarette smoke. There was a wood-burning stove in the corner, which was burning logs. The major-general looked tired with large black shadows under both eyes. His bald head seemed to shine under the electric light. He had a bulge at the rear of his skull where a silver plate had been inserted as a result of being hit with a bomb fragment during the First World War. He looked older than his fifty-eight years.

Major Fromm informed the major-general that Captain Muller had an urgent message.

Captain Muller handed him the cryptographer's note. Backhaus got up from the piano stool, put on his spectacles and read the contents. He sat still in his chair behind his desk for fully half a minute and both Major Fromm and Captain Muller knew from the expression on his face that he was a deeply troubled man.

Captain Muller informed the major-general about the Soviet air attack on the army base a short time earlier. 'There were major casualties, sir, there was carnage everywhere,' he said. 'We were taken completely by surprise.'

'And what about collateral damage?' asked Backhaus. 'Lay it on the line, Captain, how bad is it?'

The captain paused before answering; he knew the major-general wouldn't be happy. 'It's a mess, sir. We've taken hits to vehicles and infrastructure. I'm still waiting for the full report to come in, but we sustained some serious damage.'

Major-General Backhaus leaned back in his chair and took a long breath before continuing his interrogation; if he wasn't careful, he would lose his rag. 'OK, Captain Muller, did you recognise any of the attacking aircraft?'

'Yes, sir,' Muller replied. 'It all happened in a bit of a blur and they came out of nowhere, but they were unmistakable, sir: MiG-3 and LaGG-3 Soviet fighters, a whole bloody squadron.'

Major-General Backhaus lit a cigarette. He opened a drawer in his desk and removed a large book, which contained pictures of all aircraft manufactured in the Soviet Union. He went through the pages and then stopped. He turned the book round.

Captain Muller was looking at a picture of a MiG-3. The major-general then flicked the pages over and again turned the book round.

Captain Muller was looking at a LaGG-3 Soviet fighter. Major-General Backhaus said, 'These were the aircraft that you saw attack the base?'

Captain Muller replied, 'Yes, sir.'

Major-General Backhaus then opened another drawer and removed a set of compasses. He looked at the details of both aircraft and informed both officers that the MiG-3 had a range of seven hundred and seventy-six kilometres and the LaGG-3 only four hundred. He got up from his seat and walked over to a huge wall map of the Soviet Union and set the compasses at exactly two hundred kilometres. He placed one end of the compasses on the location of the army base and then drew a complete circle. The circle went through the Sea of Azov and then north of Krasnodar and was fully one hundred kilometres short of Stalingrad in the east.

The major-general said, 'Captain, when the attack took place, which direction did they come from and which direction did they leave?'

Captain Muller informed him that the aircraft had come up from the south and had gone back the same way.

The major-general pointed at the Sea of Azov on the map. He said, 'The bastards have come from a carrier. There is no other way they could have hit us. Two weeks ago intelligence informed us that an aircraft carrier had left the Black Sea fleet and now we know.'

The major-general sat down at his desk and opened a third drawer. He produced a full bottle of vodka and three glasses. He filled them to the brim. He nodded at the two officers to lift a glass each.

The major-general stood up and said, 'To the Sixth Army, gentlemen.'

All three swallowed the spirit in one go. The major-general replenished their glasses and continued to do so until the bottle was empty. He took out another and the three of them finished it in under half an hour. During this time the major-general instructed his staff officer to ascertain how much fuel would be required to move the Panzer unit, which included nearly a thousand vehicles, from Rostov to Kharkov in the Ukraine. All three knew that the Rostov base had been starved of fuel for months. A figure reached, the major-general instructed Captain Muller to send a message by Enigma to Kharkov Headquarters, seeking further instructions and requesting the requisite diesel and petrol. He was told to sign it 'Backhaus'.

Captain Muller took his leave. He felt very light-headed and when the extreme cold hit him he felt dizzy. He realised that he had consumed too much vodka to be driving the Kübelwagen. It was snowing heavily and he had to operate the windscreen wipers to see the road properly. He started to chuckle to himself at the thought of the major-general playing the piano just when the 6th Army had capitulated at Stalingrad.

The journey back to the bunker was slow as the wind was gusting and lifting the fresh snow upwards, making visibility difficult; the vodka only made matters worse.

He eventually reached the base and stopped outside the bunker. He called to a young sentry who was on duty and told him that the vehicle was extremely low on fuel and to find a petrol can and to put at least five litres in the tank. Captain Muller walked rather unsteadily across to the remains of the Nissen hut and learned that the Enigma machines had been removed to another building. He located it and approached the cryptographer, a Corporal Fritz Spinner, who was on duty. He handed the corporal a piece of paper and instructed him to send its contents forthwith to Headquarters at Kharkov. Corporal Spinner dispatched the message there and then.

At 4 a.m. a reply was received from Headquarters instructing the Rostov Panzer unit to travel to Kharkov on Wednesday 3 February and that the Luftwaffe transport aircraft would be flying in diesel and petrol to Rostov today, Monday, and tomorrow.

Corporal Spinner took the message to Captain Muller's bunker where he found the captain sound asleep on a camp bed covered with heavy blankets and a bear skin. He looked at the captain's face under torchlight and knew it wasn't going to be easy to wake him. He lit the paraffin lamp on the table and switched off his torch. He went over to Captain Muller and started to shake his shoulder. It made little difference because Muller was out cold. After several attempts, Captain Muller finally stirred and woke up.

He looked dreadful and felt dreadful.

Corporal Spinner handed him the reply from Kharkov.

Captain Muller screwed up his eyes and read the message. He told the corporal to wake him again at 6 a.m. sharp and then went back to sleep.

Corporal Spinner turned down the paraffin lamp and left.

Captain Muller was duly woken at 6 a.m. on the dot and looked just as rough as he had two hours earlier. He had a thirst and made some ersatz coffee. He drank two cups in quick succession. He dressed and donned his army greatcoat and put on a balaclava and then his military cap. He climbed the stairs from his bunker and went outside. It was pitch black and was snowing heavily. He felt awful because of the extreme cold and the shit awful vodka that he had consumed the night before. He walked to the Kübelwagen, got behind the wheel, and drove out of the army base, back towards Major-General Backhaus's dacha.

The weather had deteriorated and visibility was down to under ten metres. He was in a blizzard. At one stage he did not know whether he was on the road or in a field as everything looked the same. He was driving purely by guesswork.

Conditions were so bad that he nearly missed the turn-off to the major-general's dacha.

After going through all the identification formalities Captain Muller was taken to Major Fromm's quarters as requested.

Captain Muller knocked on the door and waited. After about twenty seconds, Muller heard movement and soon after the door was opened by a bleary-eyed Major Fromm. His monocle had hurriedly been placed over his right eye and was somewhat askew.

Major Fromm looked at Captain Muller and said, 'Ah, Muller. Come, come in.'

The room was quite small and poorly furnished. It was

also cold. There was a bed, a desk and two chairs. A telephone stood on the desk.

Major Fromm was wearing a long dressing-gown. He picked up a jug and poured some water into a glass and drank it in one go. He had a hangover and looked as rough as Captain Muller.

Muller handed him the Enigma reply received from Headquarters in Kharkov. Major Fromm sat down at his desk and rang Major-General Backhaus next door. The conversation lasted under a minute.

Major Fromm replaced the handset and looked at Captain Muller. 'The major-general instructs that we pull out the day after tomorrow. All tank crews are to service their tanks before we leave for Kharkov and any tank that breaks down due to lack of servicing will result in a court martial. Pass on that instruction when you get back to your base.'

'Major, how long will it take to travel to the base in Kharkov?'

'I have allowed twenty-four to thirty hours but it could take longer, Muller, should we have breakdowns or be attacked again by the Soviet fighters, and there is also the chance of partisan activity. God only knows.'

Captain Muller took his leave and drove back to the base at Rostov, reaching it just before 7 a.m. He entered his bunker, removed his boots and greatcoat and got into bed. He slept until 9 a.m.

Later that day, Colonel Buchalter – the major-general's deputy – assembled the one hundred and twenty tank commanders along with their crews and informed them that fuel was now arriving and that they would be leaving for Kharkov on Wednesday 3 February. All the men cheered because they had been fed up for months.

Colonel Buchalter was in his early fifties and sported a very fine crew cut. He had lost his right eye on the Somme in France during the First World War and wore a black eyepatch. He had a duelling scar that ran from the corner of his left eye to his mouth. He was feared by his subordinates and had a dreadful temper.

At midday, the huge Horch staff car drove into the Rostov base and stopped outside Colonel Buchalter's headquarters. The two pennants above the front wings, each bearing the swastika, hung limply as there was no wind. Just extreme cold. Major-General Backhaus got out of the back seat and was followed by Major Fromm. The major-general was wearing his Iron Cross, 1st Class, just below his throat. He had been awarded it for bravery on the Chemin des Dames in the Aisne region of France in 1917.

Colonel Buchalter saluted the major-general and invited him inside his headquarters where they had coffee and schnapps.

Major-General Backhaus smoked a cigarette as he spoke. The two men discussed the Stalingrad situation for about twenty minutes. Backhaus then asked the colonel to take him to the military hospital to see the wounded.

Somebody must have tipped off the senior army doctor as he was waiting at the entrance when the major-general arrived. Backhaus did not speak to any of the wounded men individually but addressed them in the various wards, telling them that they would be flown out by transport aircraft over the next two days to Kharkov and then back to the Fatherland. Some of the wounded started to clap.

The major-general then left the hospital and went to the makeshift mortuary. As he entered he started to cough badly. The senior army doctor who was with him advised him to stop smoking or seriously cut back or his condition would turn into bronchitis. The major-general simply grunted.

The total number of dead had risen to one hundred and nine, and the major-general was visibly shaken when he came out of the mortuary. He turned to Major Fromm and instructed him to get a detail ready to dig a trench forthwith and to torch the ground using petrol and wood to make the digging easier. The major-general then toured the base and examined the damage done by the Soviet fighters.

He lit a cigarette and again started to cough badly. He turned to his staff officer and said, 'One hundred and nine out of twenty-five thousand. I suppose it could have been worse, Fromm.'

They drove back to Colonel Buchalter's HQ.

Major-General Backhaus told the colonel that once all the injured had been flown out, the remaining transport planes should be filled with troops from the base and flown back to Kharkov.

The injured were flown out that afternoon. Transport planes were arriving every ten minutes and being unloaded. Troops were then boarding the aircraft for the flight to Kharkov. The last plane left Rostov under cover of darkness late Tuesday afternoon. The fuel had been delivered and nearly nine thousand soldiers had been flown back to Kharkov, leaving sixteen thousand at the Rostov base.

3

At 3 a.m. on Wednesday 3 February, Captain Muller was woken by Corporal Spinner, the duty cryptographer. The corporal handed him a message that had just been received via the Enigma machine.

Captain Muller took the paper and read that there had been a marked increase in partisan activity in the Don region of Russia and that the 4th Panzer unit should be on the alert. He told the corporal that he would see to this at 6 a.m. that morning.

Muller duly informed Colonel Buchalter and other Wehrmacht officers and shortly afterwards the one hundred and twenty Panther tanks set off in the direction of Kharkov. They were accompanied by the remaining sixteen thousand troops. The convoy included three fuel tankers; two carried diesel and the other petrol. They positioned themselves at the rear of the column so that they could fuel up any vehicle that ran dry.

Major-General Backhaus met the column at a prearranged rendezvous point.

Colonel Buchalter said to the Major General, 'Sir, we received an Enigma from Colonel Hockel at Kharkov. The message stressed that there had been a marked increase in partisan activity both in the Don region and eastern Ukraine.'

The Major General replied, 'These people can be dealt with. They are not that big a problem because they do not possess heavy armour. The only weapon that worries me is the Panzer Faust, which they have stolen from us at Stalingrad.'

The colonel caught a whiff of stale alcohol from the major-general's breath and knew that he had been at the vodka bottle the night before. As usual he had a cigarette in his mouth and was coughing badly.

Backhaus told Colonel Buchalter to get the column moving and the signal was given. The mighty Panther tanks with their huge diesel engines started to move forward.

Major-General Backhaus instructed his driver to position the Horch staff car between the first and second tanks leading the column, but after about twenty minutes the major-general started to cough again and he instructed his driver to overtake the leading tank and to lead the column himself.

Major Fromm said, 'Sir, I have seen the Enigma from Colonel Hockel and I think it is a bit risky to expose the staff car. We are a sitting duck.'

Backhaus exploded, 'I cannot sit here with these damned diesel fumes coming in. I can hardly bloody breathe.'

The driver did as he was instructed and drove past the leading tank away from the exhaust fumes. As they drove, the major-general continued to smoke and cough. Major Fromm looked miserable and was worried.

Once the whole column was on the road it stretched for several kilometres.

Soon after midday, the column had just passed through the town of Thorez when without warning the MiG-3 and LaGG-3 Soviet fighters from the aircraft carrier in the Sea of Azov came in fast and low from the east. The twelve fighters swooped one at a time, strafing the column, and the tankers at the rear were the first to be hit. The petrol tanker was stuck by cannon fire and immediately exploded into a huge fireball but amazingly the diesel tankers did not ignite.

The first fifty troop-carrying lorries were struck before the others realised what was happening. Soldiers started to scramble out of the lorries in large numbers as they knew that they were going to be hit in a matter of seconds. They got off the road and ran into the fields and started firing at the fighters with their rifles.

The tank commanders saw the Soviet fighters approaching and closed their hatches. Cannon and bullets bounced off the heavy armour but it was a different story further back as many of the Opel lorries were ablaze, with dead and dying soldiers lying beside them.

The last Soviet fighter to strafe the column was a LaGG-3, which was struck many times by the troops' firepower on the ground. Black smoke trailed from it and its engine could clearly be heard to misfire. The pilot tried to bring its nose up but without success. He brought the aircraft down on the main Rostov to Kharkov highway some two kilometres west of the column. The pilot pulled back his canopy and hauled himself out of the cockpit. He stepped on to the wing and then slid down on to the ground. He sprinted as fast as he could to the shelter of a nearby forest to make himself scarce as he knew that otherwise he faced certain death.

The remaining eleven Soviet pilots decided not to chance their luck and make a second run as the risk was too great. They flew north and then turned south away from the column.

Major-General Backhaus instructed his driver to turn round as the Horch staff car was unscathed. They drove down to the rear of the column to ascertain the situation. The major-general was appalled at what he saw. Every troop-carrying lorry had been hit with machine-gun bullets or cannon. The rear of the column had taken the brunt of the attack. Dozens of soldiers had been killed and dozens had been badly injured. Many had been burned to death in lorries that were still blazing. The situation was chaotic. The majority of the troops had managed to get out and take refuge in the fields.

The army doctors and medics were soon in attendance to treat the wounded and certify death. Troops were ordered to assist the medics with the dying and wounded who were then ferried up the column to vehicles that were still serviceable. The column did not move until some two hours after the air attack; it was now reduced to half its original size.

Every Panther tank was now crowded with troops on top. They had their greatcoats buttoned up to their necks, trying to keep warm in the freezing conditions. They looked miserable with their rifles strapped to their shoulders. Some were sobbing because they had lost friends in the attack.

The column eventually moved off but the lead tank stopped about two hundred metres from the abandoned LaGG-3 fighter, which was blocking the highway. The tank fired a shell at the aircraft and blew it to pieces. The aircraft's fuel tanks exploded into a huge fireball. The aviation fuel burnt itself out after twenty minutes and the column set off west. They were travelling at about twenty miles per hour with the major-general's Horch staff car out in front leading the column.

The major-general opened his briefcase and took out a full bottle of vodka and poured some of the spirit into a glass, which he offered to Major Fromm. Fromm declined.

Major-General Backhaus swallowed the spirit in one go and refilled his glass and put the bottle back into his briefcase.

At this time the column was about twenty kilometres west of Thorez when suddenly there was a crack from a rifle shot. The partisan sniper was concealed on a wooden railway bridge, which crossed the road. The first shot struck the front of the Horch, entering its radiator, causing severe water loss. The second hit the driver on the upper cheekbone and the third struck Major-General Backhaus above the right eye.

Major Fromm dived off his seat on to the rear footwell for cover. The Horch went out of control and slewed into a ditch and came to rest.

The tank commander in the Panther immediately behind the Horch fired a shell at the bridge, blowing it to smithereens, and the partisan's headless body was blown on to the roadway along with other debris. Both the driver of the Horch and Major-General Backhaus died instantly.

Major Fromm got out of the staff car and pulled the dead driver from his seat. He got behind the steering wheel and started up the engine. He engaged first gear and tried to drive the Horch out of the ditch but the rear wheels would not grip and kept spinning.

The tank commander climbed down from his tank and walked to where the Horch was parked. He said to Major Fromm, 'It's no use, Major, you will seize up the engine because the radiator has a hole in it and it's losing all its water.'

Major Fromm screamed at the tank commander, 'Get a cable and haul me out of this ditch and that's an order.'

Just as the tank commander was about to turn and get a cable from his tank, another Horch staff car drew up and stopped. Colonel Buchalter got out of his Horch and walked over to Major Fromm. Major Fromm did not speak. He simply turned his head and looked at the Horch staff car in the ditch.

Colonel Buchalter walked over to the stricken Horch and looked in the back and saw the body of Major-General Backhaus lying across the rear seat with part of his head missing.

At this stage, the tank commander was at the front of the stricken Horch trying to attach a cable round the bumper support.

Colonel Buchalter asked him what he was trying to do and the tank commander informed him that he had been instructed to tow the Horch to Kharkov as it was no longer driveable.

Colonel Buchalter exploded, 'Don't be such a bloody fool, Fromm. It's only a bloody staff car. Leave it. Get the major-general's body along with the driver into a lorry and, Fromm, clean your moustache and sleeve.'

Major Fromm looked at his upper left sleeve and saw shards of bone and bits of brain clinging to the material. He then looked in the wing mirror of the abandoned Horch and saw white pieces of brain clinging to his big moustache. He felt like vomiting.

He took out his handkerchief and wiped away the matter. His face was white and his monocle was dangling in front of his chest.

Major Fromm instructed two soldiers who had been riding on the lead tank to come down and remove the bodies. He then went into the rear of the abandoned Horch and removed the major-general's briefcase. He saw that it contained two bottles of vodka, Enigma codes, cigarettes and a gold fountain pen. He removed the vodka bottles and put the pen in his pocket. He took two long swigs from one of the vodka bottles and felt the spirit warming his insides as he stood on that highway in the dreadful cold. He put the bottles back in the briefcase.

At this stage Captain Muller drove up in his Kübelwagen. 'What happened, Major? I didn't see.'

Major Fromm replied, 'A sniper, Muller. He was on the bridge.'

Major Fromm ordered the two soldiers to place the two bodies in the rear of the Kübelwagen. Captain Muller turned the vehicle round and drove down the column, passing the Panther tanks until he came to the first troop-carrying lorry. He stopped next to it and ordered two soldiers out and instructed them to remove the two dead bodies from the Kübelwagen and place them in the rear of the lorry, which was occupied by fifty soldiers. The young soldiers immediately recognised that their major-general was one of the deceased. When this was done, Captain Muller turned the Kübelwagen round and drove back up the column.

Colonel Buchalter had now positioned his Horch behind the leading tank. Captain Muller stopped opposite the Horch and Major Fromm got out and informed the colonel that the major-general's body had been placed in a lorry and that the column was ready to move. Colonel Buchalter gave the leading tank the signal and the Panther tank started to move forward. After about two hundred metres its tracks went over the torso of the dead partisan crushing it beneath.

Captain Muller fell back some one hundred metres and found a space between two tanks. Major Fromm opened Major-General Backhaus's briefcase and took out the vodka bottle and handed it to the captain. Captain Muller took a long swig and handed it back.

The column had been travelling for a full two hours since the incident with the sniper. It was just after 2.30 p.m. when suddenly the leading tank was struck by an anti-tank shell, causing its offside track to come adrift.

The shell had been fired from a forest some two hundred and fifty metres from the column on the north side. Colonel Buchalter's driver immediately pulled out from the column and then reversed back as far as the fifth tank.

Colonel Buchalter shouted across, 'Muller, get back down the column and get five hundred men up here now.'

Captain Muller pulled out and drove as fast as he could past all the Panther tanks. He stopped opposite the first troop-carrying lorry and told the driver to make his way up to the leading tank. He got out of his Kübelwagen and ran down the line telling the drivers to follow the lorry in front.

The sergeants with the lorries shouted '*Raus, raus*' as the soldiers jumped from their vehicles.

Several mortars were quickly set up and soon they were firing missiles the short range into the forest. The mortars could be heard exploding as they hit the ground. Heavy machine-guns were soon firing thousands of rounds into the forest.

Another tank was struck by an anti-tank shell, which damaged the rear track drive. At this stage the tank commanders turned their tanks to face northwards and then let fly with their machine-guns. The awesome power demolished some of the trees, and the soldiers started to advance towards the forest with bayonets fixed.

Some soldiers were dropping as the partisans in the forest started to fire back.

The main thrust towards the wood was carried out by two hundred soldiers and within fifteen minutes the remaining partisans were completely surrounded. The original group had numbered about one hundred and fifty and were well equipped. Only forty of them came out of the forest alive. Some twenty-seven German soldiers had lost their lives, and some forty had been wounded. The deceased and the wounded were brought back to the column and attended to by the doctors and medics.

The forty remaining partisans were huddled together next to the column surrounded by soldiers with their bayonets pointing at them. Colonel Buchalter approached them, knowing by that time they had all been searched and disarmed. He was accompanied by a young lieutenant who was fluent in Russian. The lieutenant spoke to a male partisan who seemed to be the oldest survivor. 'Where are you from?' he asked. The hatred in the partisan's eyes was apparent to everyone. The lieutenant repeated his question and that was when the partisan spat in the lieutenant's face.

Colonel Buchalter ordered the soldiers back to their

lorries. He turned and looked at the soldiers who were manning the machine-guns and nodded.

They opened up and the partisans dropped like flies. They kept on firing until there was no sign of life.

Some of the young soldiers started to vomit after witnessing this wholesale slaughter.

A short time later a detail entered the forest and brought out weapons that had been used by the partisans. Colonel Buchalter instructed the young lieutenant to get the engineers up fast in order to repair the two damaged tanks.

The Panzer unit carried spare parts but it was over two hours later before the repairs were carried out and by that time it was pitch black.

The ten troop-carrying lorries remained near the head of the column in case there were further partisan attacks. The column set off again for Kharkov with their dead and wounded.

They finally reached Kharkov at 7 a.m. on Thursday, some twenty-five hours after leaving the Rostov base. Most of the soldiers who had been carried on the tanks were suffering from hypothermia as the temperature through the night had dropped to minus thirty degrees centigrade. Upon reaching Kharkov many of these men were hospitalised along with the wounded who were eventually flown back to Germany.

Major-General Backhaus was buried the following day in a Kharkov cemetery and was given full military honours. Many other funerals took place that day.

Major Fromm and Captain Muller both survived the war.

Major Fromm was a prisoner-of-war in a camp near his home city of Dortmund. When the bank manager of the Deutsche Bank where Fromm had worked before the war informed the senior British officer in charge of the camp that Fromm was an employee and had never been a member of the Nazi party, Fromm was duly released. After being treated for malnutrition and other medical problems for two months he returned to work at the bank.

Captain Muller was also released and eventually rejoined the new West German army in 1949 and rose up through the ranks before retiring.

Part 2

4

Calum Breffit was born in Tallinn, Estonia. He was the only son of the British Consul. His mother was Estonian and Calum was bilingual – in English and Russian. He returned to England when he was seven years of age and attended an infant school in the village of Ringmer near Lewes in East Sussex where his parents had bought a large house. His father worked at the Foreign Office and only came home at weekends as he had a flat in Maida Vale, London.

Eventually Calum went to study at Lancing College in West Sussex. When he was sixteen years old, he walked into the boys' toilet where there were two other boys smoking a cannabis joint. A master came in and caught them. Calum protested his innocence and told the master that he had only come in to use the urinal. All three were at first suspended and then expelled. Calum's father appealed but to no avail. He told Calum that he would send him to another fee-paying school but Calum had already contacted a Rolls-Royce/Bentley garage with a view to starting an apprenticeship. His father eventually relented and Calum became an apprentice motor mechanic, a job which he loved. By the age of twenty-one he was a fully time-served mechanic.

Shortly after this time Calum bought his own flat just off the Seven Dials in Brighton. He started to suffer from dermatitis and when his condition got worse he sought help from his doctor. His doctor told him that his condition was due to contact with oil and advised Calum to change his career. Calum left the garage much to the disappointment of its owner and took up employment as a roustabout on a North Sea oil rig after undergoing a survival course.

After a year he became a roughneck and the following year an assistant driller. Two years on and he was a driller, a highly paid post. He was just twenty-seven years of age.

Calum had just finished a fourteen-day tour of duty on the rig when he, along with others, was waiting to be picked up by helicopter and taken back to Dyce Airport near Aberdeen. The wind was nearing gale force and the approaching helicopter was getting buffeted by the wind.

The chopper aborted its first attempt to land and had to go round the rig for a second attempt. It landed heavily on the helipad. Fourteen men alighted and fourteen men boarded.

Calum was seated immediately behind the two pilots. The helicopter took off and after about twenty minutes the aircraft started to vibrate. Calum noticed red lights appearing on the dashboard. The co-pilot shouted to the men to assume crash positions as they were going to ditch in the sea.

Calum could hear the pilot shouting into his mouthpiece: 'Mayday, mayday...' He also gave his approximate position. As the helicopter touched water the two flotation air bags at each side of the craft inflated automatically to prevent it from sinking. Two large dinghies were deployed and also inflated. The men, who were wearing survival suits, clambered into them. The sea was rough and they were being tossed about like corks. Calum had never been so scared in all his life.

The pilot was in one inflatable whilst the co-pilot was in the other. They both assured the men that they would be rescued as soon as the coastguard had received the Mayday message.

After about twenty-five minutes an RAF Sea King helicopter was seen approaching. The winchman came down and brought up all sixteen men and flew them to Dyce Airport.

The Press were there in numbers but Calum walked past them. He went into the gents' and splashed cold water over his face. He looked in the mirror and his eyes told him that he'd had a scare. He vowed there and then that he would never board another helicopter.

He caught a flight to Gatwick and then a train to Brighton. He then took a taxi to the Seven Dials and went into a nearby pub where he had a pint of real ale. He saw a customer reading an *Evening Argus* and recognised a column about the helicopter crash. Calum returned to his flat and opened a bottle of merlot. He sat down in front of his computer and surfed the Web for shore-based jobs in the oil industry.

One job caught his eye. It read:

Wanted urgently – executive with drilling experience who is fluent in both English and Russian to work in Baku, Azerbaijan. Send CV by e-mail.

Calum sent off his CV and an acknowledgement was received within the hour saying that another would be sent later that day. About two hours later he received it; he had been asked to come to Houston, Texas, for an interview. He was to go to Heathrow Airport on the coming Monday and pick up his flight tickets from the British Airways desk. This gave Calum two days before his flight.

He went to bed early and rose early the next day. He went to his rented garage and took out his 1958 MGA sports car. He drove to the police traffic base at Hickstead where his best friend, Roger Brooks, was a motorcyclist. When they met the first thing Roger asked him was whether he had been on the helicopter that had ditched in the sea.

Calum nodded. 'I was. I was sitting right behind both pilots. I knew something was wrong when the chopper started to vibrate and when I saw a lot of lights suddenly appear on the dashboard. I thought, Christ, we are in trouble. To be honest, Roger, I thought my time was up. It was really scary. The pilots were absolutely brilliant. They got the chopper down in just a few seconds, otherwise we would have been killed. I will never ever fly in another paraffin budgie. Once bitten, twice shy.'

Roger sympathised and then Calum said, 'I'm going to Houston on Monday for an interview and I'll phone you when I get back.'

Calum went back to his flat and wrote out his resignation to the company who had employed him as a driller. He gave his reasons. He was sure that the company would accept them.

On the Monday morning Calum caught the train to Victoria and then got a connection to Heathrow. He picked up his flight tickets at the British Airways desk. He boarded the aircraft and was ushered into business class. He had a meal but abstained from alcohol during the flight. He got off the plane at Houston and immediately felt the heat of the sun.

He passed through customs and was heading to the exit to get a taxi when he spotted a tall black man holding a large board above his head sporting the name 'Mr Breffit'.

Calum approached the man who introduced himself as Virgil Johnson, chauffeur to the chairman of Temco International Oil Company. They both walked out of the airport and headed towards the parking lot.

They drove out of the lot in Virgil's Lincoln and onto the freeway for about two miles before turning off. They entered a tree-lined boulevard and it was at this point that Calum spotted a 1952 Rolls-Royce Silver Dawn, which was three cars in front, stopped at traffic lights.

When the lights changed to green the Rolls-Royce moved off and it was then that Calum noticed a lot of steam coming from its exhaust pipe. Calum turned to Virgil and said, 'The

Rolls-Royce in front has a serious engine problem and I suspect it has blown a cylinder-head gasket. Just look at the steam coming out of the exhaust pipe.'

Virgil said, 'Are you sure, sir?'

'I should be,' replied Calum, 'I'm a qualified Rolls-Royce mechanic.'

Virgil did not reply. He put his foot to the floor. He passed two cars in front and then overtook the Rolls-Royce, which was being driven by a white-haired elderly gentleman.

Virgil put his hazard lights on and the Rolls-Royce stopped. Virgil got out of the Lincoln and walked quickly to the Rolls-Royce and spoke to the driver. The driver switched off the engine. Calum joined them by the Silver Dawn. It was immaculate in metallic green. The driver pulled the bonnet catch and Virgil opened up one side. He slowly unscrewed the cap at the top of the radiator and looked in to find that there was no water in the top part of the radiator. Calum looked at the temperature gauge and saw that the needle was right up at 'H'.

Calum told the elderly gentleman that he thought the Rolls-Royce had been stopped in time and that the engine should be all right once it had been topped up with water.

Half an hour later the car was fixed and ready to go though Calum told the owner that the head gasket would need to be looked at. He would stop and help further but he had a job interview at Temco International Oil Company in half an hour and had better dash.

The old man smiled and thanked him profusely, asking whether he was a mechanic.

Calum said, 'Yes, I served my apprenticeship with a Rolls-Royce garage in Sussex and was fully qualified before I went offshore.'

The elderly gentleman shook Calum's hand and then drove off.

Calum looked at Virgil who had a silly grin on his face.

Virgil drove for another two miles and turned off the boulevard into San Antonio Avenue. Calum recognised the name and knew that he was near to Temco International Oil Company HQ. They turned off the avenue into a parking lot next to a glass skyscraper. Virgil parked up and Calum got out of the Lincoln. He then spotted the Rolls-Royce Silver Dawn in the parking lot.

Virgil by this time had a huge grin on his face. He took Calum's holdall and they walked to the front of the building. Virgil spoke to a security guard at the door and the pair of them entered. Calum was taken to a ground-floor bathroom where he had a wash and clean up. He took off his shirt and put on a fresh one as he had been sweating in the heat. Virgil then took him to the elevator and pressed the button for the twelfth floor. They got out and entered a large office where the receptionist was sitting behind her desk.

Virgil informed the secretary that Mr Breffit's appointment with the president was at 2 p.m. Virgil took his leave but just before he did he turned round and said, 'Mr Breffit, good luck, sir.'

Calum sat in an easy chair and waited. The secretary looked at him and smiled. She was very attractive, Nordic-looking, with beautiful blue eyes.

Calum was just about to speak when the phone buzzed. He looked at his watch. It was two exactly. The receptionist picked up the handset and then replaced it. She got up from her desk and walked over to another door, which she opened. She looked at Calum and beckoned him to enter the president's office. As he passed her she winked at him. Calum entered the room, which was huge. He immediately saw three men sitting behind a very large desk and in the middle was the driver of the Rolls-Royce Silver Dawn.

The elderly gentleman said, 'Take a seat, Mr Breffit, I would just like to thank you again for saving my Rolls-Royce engine from seizing up.' The two men flanking the president stared at each other.

The president then told them what had happened and how he had been stopped by his chauffeur. Next, he introduced himself. 'I am Arnold Huber, President of Temco and this is my company secretary and director for Europe and South East Asia.'

Calum had a gut feeling that he was about to get the third degree.

Mr Huber said, 'What do you know about Temco International, Mr Breffit?'

Calum replied, 'Sir, I do not know anything about your company. I saw your advert on the internet and applied for the post in Azerbaijan as I feel that I am qualified.'

Mr Huber said, 'This company has interests worldwide and employs many hundreds of people. How long have you worked in the oil industry?'

'About six years, sir. I started off in the North Sea as a Roustabout and then became a Roughneck, Assistant Driller and finally Driller.'

'A Driller on a rig is a very well-paid position. Why did you decide to give it all up?' asked Mr Huber.

'I came off the rig because I nearly lost my life in a helicopter which was forced to ditch in the sea,' Calum replied.

Mr Huber sat up in his seat and leaned forward. 'What was wrong with the chopper?'

'The main shaft in the gearbox was seizing up and the pilots only had seconds to ditch or we would all have perished.'

Mr Huber said, 'You were very lucky, young man. Now, let's see how your Russian is.' He picked up his telephone and spoke briefly to his secretary. A few seconds later, Igor Mankovich, a Russian-speaking employee, entered the room.

'Right, Igor. I want you to ask Mr Breffit some questions in Russian and give me your opinion.'

Igor Mankovich spoke to Calum for fully two minutes and asked him several questions, which Calum answered easily.

'Well, Igor,' said Mr Huber, 'how good is he?'

'He is very good, sir, I cannot fault him. His accent is from the Baltic region.'

Mr Huber asked Calum, 'How did you come to speak fluent Russian, Mr Breffit?'

'I was born in Tallinn in Estonia, sir. My mother was a native of Tallinn but my father was British. In fact, he was the British Consul in that city. I was seven years of age when we returned to England and by that time I was fluent in Russian and English. My mother would always speak to me in Russian and still does.'

Mr Huber said, 'Your parents now live in England?'

Calum replied, 'Yes, sir, they live in a small village a few miles north of Brighton. My father now works at the Foreign Office and comes home at weekends.'

Mr Huber said, 'Very interesting. Now, Mr Breffit, if you would be good enough to take a seat outside in the secretary's office.' Calum and the secretary smiled at each other. About five minutes later the phone rang which the secretary answered. She replaced the handset, got up and walked over and opened the door to Mr Huber's office. She beckoned to Calum. As Calum passed her she whispered 'Moment of truth' and winked at him again.

Calum went back into the office and Mr Huber said to him, 'We are prepared to offer you the position of executive in Baku, Azerbaijan. When can you start?'

Calum said, 'Sir, I will need to return to Brighton to sort out a few loose ends, and visit my parents.'

Mr Huber said, 'That's fine, young man, but I want you back here within a week as you will be attending various drilling companies here in Houston to learn all the latest techniques before taking up your new post in Baku.'

'I'll be back within a week, sir. Mr Huber, my flight to London does not leave until eleven tonight. I would be happy to repair your Silver Dawn, as I have worked on them many times before.'

'Thanks, Calum, you're a sport,' said Mr Huber and he left him to his task of fixing up his prized automobile.

After fixing the Rolls, Calum went back into the Temco building to clean up. Then Virgil took him to the canteen as both of them were getting hungry. Calum saw Mr Huber's secretary sitting at a table on her own. He went over to her and asked if he could join her. She smiled and asked him how he had got on.

Calum replied with a smile, 'I have been appointed to the post in Baku.'

Traudel's eyes lit up. 'I am so pleased. I was hoping that you were going to get it.'

Calum could not take his eyes off her. He really fancied this tall blonde. He said, 'I have a flight at eleven but I'll be back within a week.' They spoke for about an hour and then he had to leave. She wished him a safe flight and left and it was only then that he realised he had never even asked her her name.

At the airport, Virgil handed Calum an envelope, which he said was from Mr Huber. Calum opened it and found that it contained a one thousand-dollar bill. Calum told Virgil to stay where he was and that he would be back in a couple of minutes. He walked over to a bureau de change and changed the bill for two five hundreds. He put one back into the envelope and handed it to Virgil.

Virgil said, 'I can't take this, Mr Breffit.'

Calum replied, 'Virgil, I could not have repaired the Rolls without your help. Now put that in your pocket and no arguments.' He shook Virgil's hand and went into the departure lounge to await his flight.

39

5

When he got back to his flat he picked up his mail from behind the door. Among the letters was one from his old firm accepting his resignation and wishing him well for the future. They also added that if he required a reference they would only be too happy to oblige. They enclosed his P45 and said that his salary had been paid into his bank account. Calum went to bed early but had difficulty getting to sleep because he couldn't get Mr Huber's secretary out of his head. He didn't think she was married as she had not been wearing a wedding or engagement ring.

The following morning he took out his MGA and drove to Roger's flat in Kemp Town where he told him about the trip to Houston and that he was returning there the following Tuesday for one month before taking up his new job in Baku, Azerbaijan.

The following day, Calum got an e-mail from Houston telling him to pick up his flight tickets from the British Airways desk at Heathrow and that his company apartment where he would be staying would be ready for him; also that Virgil Johnson would pick him up from Houston the following Tuesday.

Arrangements had been made for Roger to check the flat once a week and to forward any mail that looked important. Calum caught the flight to Houston and arrived there at 8 p.m. He was met by Virgil and was taken in the Lincoln to an apartment block about half a mile from Temco HQ.

They both entered the building and took the elevator to

40

the second floor. Virgil had the keys and opened the apartment door. Calum was surprised how big it was. There was a large lounge, two bedrooms, bathroom and kitchen. Virgil told him that the fridge and freezer had been stocked that day and wished him a good night's rest.

Calum found a bottle of bourbon in one of the cupboards and cans of lager in the fridge. He had a couple of drinks and went to bed. He slept like a log.

The following morning, after a shower, shave and breakfast, Calum opened the apartment door only to find Mr Huber's secretary coming out of the apartment opposite.

She said, 'Good morning, Mr Breffit. I hope you had a good flight.' She stuck out her hand and added, 'I am Traudel Fromm.'

Calum took her hand and shook it.

'Right, let's head to the office,' she said.

They both got into the elevator and Calum detected a strong smell of perfume, which he recognised immediately – it was the only scent his mother ever used.

'Chanel Number Nineteen,' he said.

'You recognise the scent. Well you are the first man who has ever told me what perfume I am wearing.'

They reached the bottom and the pair of them got out of the elevator and walked out into very strong sunlight. They walked slowly to Temco HQ and by the time they reached the glass building they were on first name terms. This was the first time in Calum's life that he felt good in female company. He'd had girlfriends in the past but Traudel was something special.

When they reached the Temco HQ and saw Mr Huber's Rolls-Royce in the parking lot, Traudel told Calum that all the staff knew he had repaired the president's car because it was the talk of the canteen.

As they entered the building Traudel introduced Calum to two security guards. He was taken away by one and photographed and returned about five minutes later with an identification card, which contained his photograph and signature.

Traudel informed him that Mr Huber wanted to have a word with him before he got started and they both went up in the elevator to her office.

Traudel knocked on Mr Huber's door and went in. She reappeared and told Calum to go in. Calum entered the huge office and saw Mr Huber sitting behind his desk.

Mr Huber got up and shook Calum's hand and asked him if he had settled in all right. Calum assured him he had.

Mr Huber told Calum to take a seat.

'Right, Calum, down to business. You are here to learn all aspects of being an oil executive and you must remember that when you are out in Baku and a problem develops it is your responsibility to sort it out and sort it out quickly because we cannot afford to shut down an oil rig. So what I am saying to you is that when things go wrong the buck stops with you.'

Mr Huber then retrieved a blue file from his desk, which he handed to Calum. 'If you open the file you will see the programme that you will undertake over the next four weeks before you move to Baku.'

Calum opened the file and saw that over the next seven days he would be working at Temco. He would then attend other large companies in Houston involved in the manufacturing of oil tools, drills and drill bits. At the last company he was to visit he would learn about seabed and downhole technologies, drilling techniques and trouble-shooting.

Calum closed the file.

Mr Huber said, 'Are there any problems, Calum?'

'No, sir, everything seems straightforward.'

'Good. Any problems whatsoever, come up and knock on this door. Now, young man, off you go and get stuck in.'

Calum got up and walked to the door. As he did so, he turned round and said to Mr Huber, 'Mr Huber, thank you for the thousand-dollar bill.'

'You mean the five hundred-dollar bill. You see, Virgil tells me everything and what you did was commendable. You should go far, young man.'

Calum left Mr Huber's office and saw Traudel sitting at her desk in front of a display unit. Calum handed her his file and told her that this was his workload for the next four weeks.

During his time at Temco Calum would often meet Traudel for lunch and they would sit together in the canteen and talk before heading out for a walk. The time started to fly and before he knew it Calum had only two weeks left before he went out to Azerbaijan. So they made the most of their time together, enjoying each other's company each lunchtime and in the evenings. Calum made a great impression when he offered to tune up Traudel's prized VW Beetle. The car was around thirty-five years old with no rust to be seen, but it needed a little TLC under the bonnet.

By the time Calum was finished with it, it was running like a Swiss watch. When Traudel drove Calum back to the apartment block that evening she couldn't believe it was the same car. When they reached the apartment block Traudel gave Calum a kiss on the lips.

That night they had a couple of drinks in Traudel's apartment and got talking about the Alamo. Traudel told him that the old fort was near San Antonio, which she reckoned was about a hundred and fifty miles west of Houston. She asked him if he would like to visit the place and Calum told her he would. She suggested they could go the coming Saturday and that they should make the journey in three hours.

The following evening Traudel took Calum to meet her parents in Houston. He was introduced to her father, Horst, and her mother, Ingrid. Calum saw the strong resemblance between Traudel and her mother: they were both blonde for a start.

Her parents made Calum very welcome. Her father spoke English with a slight German accent but her mother sounded all American.

Horst told Calum that Ingrid had emigrated from Tromsø in Norway along with her parents and that he had followed his cousin from Dortmund in Germany. He said that he had worked in an aircraft factory before moving to Houston and opening an ironmonger's business.

Traudel saw Calum looking at a picture on a table. She told Calum that the photo was taken in Dortmund some fifteen years earlier. She pointed with her finger and said, 'There is Mom, here is Pop and next to me is grandfather Otto.'

Calum noticed that the grandfather was very tall and slim and that he was wearing a monocle and had a huge moustache like Franz Josef.

Horst asked, 'Where in England are you from, Calum?' Calum replied, 'I am from Brighton. It's a city about fifty miles south of London, on the coast.'

Horst got off his seat and opened a cupboard and produced a full bottle of twenty-year-old Macallan malt whisky. He put four glasses on the table and poured before handing the glasses round. Calum sipped the whisky and knew straightaway that he was sampling his favourite. He knew all about the Macallan as he had once visited the distillery in Banffshire. He told Horst, 'The distillery where the Macallan is made is the only one to import sherry barrels from Jerez in Spain and that is why there's a hint of sherry in the taste.' Horst listened intently.

Later Calum and Traudel returned to the apartment block and he told her that it was his turn to provide the drinks so they went to his place. They sat on the sofa and chatted away for nearly two hours, sipping beers. At the end of the evening Calum saw Traudel to her apartment and thanked her for introducing him to her parents. She kissed him on the lips and closed the door.

On the Saturday they drove to the Alamo and saw the old fort. On their way back they stopped at a diner before returning to Houston.

Calum was starting his fourth week on the Monday when he was summoned to Mr Huber's office. Mr Huber said, 'Take a seat young man.' He picked up some papers on his desk. 'I have here all the reports from the various drilling and oil tool companies that you have visited and I have never seen such glowing feedback on an employee. When you were interviewed for the Baku position I knew you had talent and that was why you were appointed in the first place. As a reward for your hard work, I am going to allow you seven days back in the UK at company expense.'

Calum said, 'Thank you, sir. My parents will be delighted.'

Mr Huber then said, 'I get the impression that you and my secretary are very close.'

'Yes, sir, I am very fond of Traudel,' replied Calum. 'Would it be possible to grant Traudel a week's leave, as I would like to take her to England to meet my parents before I leave for Azerbaijan? I would pay her fare, of course.'

Mr Huber replied, 'That will not be necessary.' He opened a drawer and handed Calum an envelope, which Calum opened. Inside were two return tickets to London's Heathrow.

'Sir, I am lost for words,' said Calum.

Mr Huber replied, 'Well, Calum, I will just have to tell her myself. She has been a very good employee and in this company good employees get rewarded.'

Later that day Calum met Traudel outside the front entrance. Calum said, 'Did Mr Huber tell you anything, Traudel?'

'Yes he did, Calum,' she replied. Calum noticed tears in her eyes. He took her hand and squeezed it. As they walked off hand in hand, Calum looked back and saw Mr Huber on the twelfth floor looking out of the window.

They reached their block and went into Traudel's apartment. Traudel put her arms round Calum's neck and kissed him fully on the lips. Calum held her close and didn't want her to let go. He knew deep down that he was falling for this beautiful Texan blonde.

6

They flew out from Houston the following Monday and arrived in London the same day. From Victoria station they caught a train to Brighton. Calum had phoned his pal Roger from Victoria and Roger told him he would be waiting for them at Brighton.

'When they arrived Roger was there as he'd promised, waiting for them on the platform. He was quickly introduced to Traudel and then he picked up her small suitcase. They told Roger that they were both jet-lagged and wanted to sleep.

Roger drove them to Calum's flat and dropped them off. They slept for a couple of hours and then went out for a meal. They came back at around eleven and went to bed. At 4 a.m. Calum woke to find Traudel lying next to him. He put his arms round her and cuddled her.

The following day Calum took his MGA out of the lock-up garage. There was not a cloud in the sky and the sun was shining. Calum took the hood down and they drove into town.

They walked down to the seafront and Calum pointed out the Grand Hotel. He said, 'That hotel was blown up by the IRA when the Prime Minister, Margaret Thatcher, was staying.'

Traudel said, 'I was little at the time but I remember my parents talking about it.'

They both sat on a bench on the seafront, watching the waves breaking on the shore. Calum took Traudel's hand and squeezed it gently. He looked into her gorgeous light blue eyes and said, 'Traudel Fromm, I love you and want to marry you. I want you to be my wife.'

Traudel replied, 'Nothing would make me happier. I fell in love with you when you first walked into my office.'

They headed back to the car hand-in-hand, then drove to Lewes, where they found a jewellers. Calum told Traudel to select an engagement ring.

She asked him about the price.

He told her not to worry. Calum had a healthy bank account especially for a twenty-seven-year-old.

Traudel selected a large diamond solitaire, which cost four figures. The band was too big for Traudel's finger and the jeweller told them to come back the following day when the ring would be ready.

Traudel was so happy. When they got back to the car she kissed Calum in thanks.

They collected the engagement ring the next day and then drove to Ringmer to see Calum's mother. Traudel got a big surprise when she saw the size of Calum's parents' house. She thought it was a mansion.

Traudel and Mrs Breffit hit it off straightaway. When Calum told his mother that he was now engaged to Traudel, she said, 'My Calum, you are always full of surprises.' She gave each of them a kiss on the cheek.

Calum said, 'We'll be back on Saturday to see Dad. Bye Mum.'

They returned to Ringmer on the Saturday morning and Traudel met Calum's father who was certainly taken with his future daughter-in-law.

On the Sunday evening they booked into a hotel at Heathrow Airport as they had an early morning flight to catch.

At Houston they were met by Virgil Johnson who took them both to the apartment block. They had an early night as they were a little jet-lagged.

The following day Traudel went to her office. Mr Huber walked past her desk and noticed the engagement ring on her finger.

'How was your break in England, Traudel?' he asked.

'Absolutely marvellous,' she replied. A few minutes later he buzzed through to Traudel and she entered his office.

The old man got up and said, 'Traudel, I want to be one of the first to congratulate you on your engagement to Calum.'

'Thank you Mr Huber.'

Mr Huber kissed Traudel on the cheek and continued: 'You have picked the right guy, my dear. He will go far in life.'

The following day Calum packed for his flight to Azerbaijan. He didn't want to leave his fiancée but he knew he had to. Virgil Johnson took both of them to the airport where Calum embraced Traudel and told her he would phone her every day.

The tears were streaming down Traudel's cheek. Even Virgil had a lump in his throat. He handed Calum an envelope from Mr Huber. Calum put it in his pocket and boarded the plane, which was Moscow bound.

Once on board, Calum opened the envelope. It contained a letter from Mr Huber and a gold American Express card in his name. In the letter Mr Huber said there was no limit on the card but not to go mad with it as it had happened before. He was told to use the card for flights and any other incidental expenses like hotels. Mr Huber said that his first tour of duty would be for six weeks and then he would have a break of two weeks.

Calum saw that the aircraft was three quarters full and that it contained mainly businessmen from both the United States and Asia.

It was 4 p.m. local time when he landed at Moscow's main airport. He was glad to have taken his father's old

Crombie overcoat to keep out the chill. He booked into an airport hotel and put his luggage in his bedroom before he descended to the bar. The bar was reasonably quiet and he went up to the barman and asked for a beer in Russian.

He then went over to a table and sat down. He noticed a pile of newspapers on another table including a day-old *Washington Post*. He picked it up and went back to his seat and started to read. After a while he noticed two blonde-haired women enter the bar. They were wearing skirts that only just covered their bottoms. They bought their drinks and then walked towards where Calum was sitting. They sat down opposite him and started to talk in Russian.

Calum kept reading his paper but was listening to their conversation.

One of the prostitutes said to her friend, 'What a nice-looking guy. He will make a nice client for the night for one hundred dollars.'

The other prostitute said to Calum, 'Would you like to take us up to your bedroom?' in broken English.

Calum replied in Russian. 'I would love to take you upstairs, but you see I am HIV positive and there is a good chance that I will pass on the virus.'

The two prostitutes quickly drank up and left.

Calum ordered another drink and the barman said, 'Were you propositioned by that pair of bitches?'

'Yes, but I told them I was HIV positive and they buggered off.'

The barman burst out laughing. 'Those bitches are regulars and I am certain that some of the management are getting backhanders from them.'

Calum retired to his room and turned in early. His flight for Baku left at 11.15 the next morning.

Calum boarded the Russian aircraft at 10.30 a.m. It was twin engined and looked like it had been in service for some years as the passenger seats were beginning to show signs of wear. The aircraft was about half full and Calum presumed that most of the male passengers were Russians returning to the oil rigs in the Caspian Sea. There was a lot of cloud for the first two hours but as the aircraft approached the Kavkaz mountains the cloud suddenly disappeared and Calum could see the ground. He looked to his left and saw the Caspian Sea, which stretched as far as the eye could see.

The aircraft was flying at thirty-five thousand feet when Calum felt it starting its descent.

7

At Baku Airport, which was relatively small compared with Moscow, Calum produced his passport. The official looked at the visa and handed it back to him. He picked up his case from the conveyor belt after a short wait and left the airport building hoping to get a taxi.

He had been standing for about two minutes when he was approached by a short, slim, dark-haired woman in her mid-thirties.

'Excuse me, but are you Mr Breffit?' she asked in English.

Calum replied in Russian that he was.

'I am Natasha Starovoitova, and I am your secretary at Temco's Baku office.' Calum stuck out his hand and Natasha shook it. She told him that the car was in the car park.

Calum picked up his case and followed her to a red Lada Riva. She opened the boot and Calum put his case in. He put his Crombie overcoat on top and closed the lid. He got into the front passenger seat and they drove off.

When they reached the outskirts of the city, Calum was stunned by its size. 'I never knew Baku was so big,' he said to Natasha.

'Oh yes,' she replied. 'There are over one million people living here.'

They drove east and then south. Calum spotted a Mercedes-Benz car showroom and then a BMW equivalent.

Calum said, 'I see that the Germans have their car showrooms in Baku. There must be a lot of money in this part of the world.'

Natasha replied, 'Since the break-up of the Soviet Union,

Azerbaijan – and Baku in particular – has become much wealthier. We no longer send money to Moscow as we are independent now.'

After about another twenty minutes, Natasha drove into a drab looking industrial estate and stopped in the car park in front of a small office block. Calum noticed the name Temco International Oil Company above the front door.

Natasha got out of the car and Calum followed. He went to the rear of the Lada but Natasha told him to leave his luggage as she would be running him to his apartment.

They entered the small two-floor building and went into a large ground-floor office where a woman sat in front of a visual display unit.

Natasha introduced Calum to Alicia Chechento, an employee of Temco.

Calum shook her hand. She had jet-black hair and he guessed she was probably local. Calum spotted the coffee pot, which was half full, and helped himself.

He chatted away to the two women for fully half an hour in Russian. They had never heard a westerner speak such perfect Russian; they were very impressed. Calum noticed the text on the visual display units, which was in Russian: one of them detailed the daily output of oil coming from the various rigs in the Caspian Sea; the other was concerned with the availability of oil tools from various manufacturers.

Natasha looked at her watch. 'Mr Breffit, are you ready to be taken to your apartment?'

'Yes, Natasha. It has been a very long day and I would like to lie down and relax.'

They both got into the Lada and Calum asked, 'Is this your own car?'

'No, sir. This is the property of Temco. We call it the office car.'

Calum asked, 'Who else is employed here?'

'There are two others whom you will meet tomorrow.

Pyotr Skuratov, a geologist from Moscow, and Anatoly Savostyanov, the messenger boy. Your predecessor referred to him as a gofer.'

'My predecessor,' Calum responded, 'I never met him. What was he like?'

Natasha said, 'He was an American from Houston in Texas who had worked at the Baku office for about eighteen months. About two months ago an email came through from Mr Huber telling him to return to Houston on the next flight available.'

Calum said, 'And he flew back to the United States?'

'Yes, he left the next day and never came back. Nobody knew the reason for his quick departure but we eventually learned from Igor Mankovich, who replaced him on a temporary basis, that he had spent over thirty thousand dollars using his Amex card and had been flying to Volgograd and other places at weekends and living it up in hotels. There was a strong rumour that he had been involved with prostitutes.'

Calum said, 'Did you ever find out what happened to him when he returned to Houston?'

Natasha replied, 'By all accounts, Mr Huber fired him and cut the Amex card in two, writing off the money.'

Natasha turned the ignition key and the Lada burst into life. She drove out of the car park and headed in the direction of the Caspian Sea, which was about four miles away. Calum could see it clearly as they were on high ground. A few minutes later they stopped outside an apartment block, similar to the one in Houston except this one contained six apartments, not twelve.

Calum removed his luggage from the boot and followed Natasha inside. There was no lift. They walked up the stairs to the first landing. Natasha took out a key ring, which had two keys. She opened the apartment door and went in, followed by Calum. The apartment was identical to the one in Houston. He mentioned this to Natasha and she told him that all Temco apartments were alike.

Calum went through to the kitchen and opened the fridge to find it was stocked. The drinks cupboard was also full but this time with local brew.

Just as Natasha was leaving she told Calum that Pyotr was in the flat opposite. Alicia was above him and she and Anatoly were on the ground floor. She said there was an empty apartment opposite Alicia. If he had any problems he had four doors to knock on.

The following morning Calum was introduced to Anatoly and Pyotr. Pyotr was thirty-one years old and had been a geologist for seven years. He had been with Temco for the last three. He wore spectacles halfway down his nose and looked like an absent-minded professor. He had an infectious laugh. Anatoly was nineteen and had been with Temco for some eighteen months. He was from Batumi in Georgia where his parents still lived. He was a happy-go-lucky type with a ready smile on his face. The five of them walked the one kilometre to the Temco office. Natasha had left the Lada in the car park at Temco the previous evening and did not use it to go to work.

Calum's office was on the top floor. He had a lap-top computer on his desk, a telephone and a mobile phone. There was a large filing cabinet in the corner, which contained the names of all personnel employed by Temco on the oil rigs in the Caspian Sea. Calum went through the files and saw that most of the workers, roustabouts and roughnecks were from Azerbaijan but some were from Volgograd, Rostov, Kharkov and Moscow. The rig supervisors were mainly from the United States and the United Kingdom.

The telephone rang at 8.15 a.m. and Calum answered in Russian: 'Temco International.'

The voice at the other end said, 'Calum?'

'Traudel! I miss you dreadfully, darling. I have been thinking about you most of the time.'

'Me too. How are you settling in, Calum?'

'Fine, I've moved into one of Temco's apartments and it is identical to the one in Houston. There are four other members of staff in the same apartment block and they are all very friendly. I am just beginning to find my feet but I have settled in OK. No problems so far.'

Traudel replied, 'Stick with it, darling, and keep yourself busy and the six weeks will pass quickly. I can't wait to be in your arms again.'

'I can't wait either,' Calum replied.

The first week dragged. In the evenings he would take a walk and go down to a nearby hotel and have a drink and listen to the locals chatting, but he did not get involved himself. Sometimes he had difficulty in understanding the local dialect.

He phoned Traudel at her apartment every day and wondered whether Mr Huber would mention the phone bill when he got back to the States.

He completed his first tour of duty in Azerbaijan and was happy that no serious problems had arisen on any of Temco's oil rigs in the Caspian Sea. He made it a priority to introduce himself to new crews going out to the rigs and to others coming back.

He would tell the Russian-speaking oilmen of his experiences in the North Sea, which seemed to impress them. The new Baku executive had not always been a white-collar worker but had once worn overalls and had got his hands dirty sometime during his career. This made him popular and the fact that he spoke perfect Russian certainly helped.

He stressed to his workforce that if they had any problems to contact him and he would help them out.

After six weeks Calum got a flight to Moscow but he missed his connecting flight to Houston because of a delay at Baku Airport. By the time he arrived in Moscow he had missed the flight and was forced to book into the same hotel for the night.

He went to the bar for a drink where the same barman recognised him. He smiled and asked Calum how he was. Calum told him he was tired but otherwise fine. He asked for a beer, which the barman served him, and went over to find a table. He sat down and picked up a *Washington Post* and started to read.

About half an hour later the two prostitutes who had propositioned him six weeks earlier entered the bar. They bought their drinks and walked towards Calum who hadn't noticed them. They sat down in front of him. Calum dropped his newspaper and they both immediately recognised him. They both got up and walked out of the bar.

The barman could hardly contain himself with laughter; he came over and put a beer next to the one Calum was drinking.

'That was so funny, sir. Please have this one on the house. That pair of bitches must keep the Malaysian rubber industry in full employment.'

Calum thanked him for the beer and continued to read his newspaper before calling it a night. As he left, the barman acknowledged his 'goodnight' with a huge grin.

The next day Calum caught a flight to Houston and arrived in the afternoon. He was met at the airport as usual by Virgil Johnson who carried his case to the waiting Lincoln.

Virgil asked Calum how the trip had been and Calum told him that there had been no problems but the six weeks had somewhat dragged and that he had missed his fiancée very much. He said that he had missed his flight because he was late in getting to Moscow.

At Temco Headquarters Calum walked into the building and took the elevator to the twelfth floor. He walked into Traudel's office and saw her sitting at her desk. She looked up and saw Calum standing there. She got up from her seat and Calum could see tears in her eyes. He put his arms around her and kissed her hard on the lips.

'That was the longest six weeks of my life,' he said.

'I have missed you so much, Calum, she replied.

Calum still had Traudel in his arms when he turned round and saw Mr Huber standing at his office door. He was smiling.

'So the lovers are back together,' he said. 'It is a lovely sight. When you have a minute, Calum, I would like a word.'

Calum released Traudel and walked into Mr Huber's office and closed the door.

Mr Huber said, 'Well, Calum, how have things been in Baku over the past six weeks?'

Calum replied, 'Sir, I did not experience any problems whatsoever. Temco's oil rigs have been operating normally and oil production has been steady. All the crews employed at Temco seem to be happy.'

'Have you met any of the crews?'

'Yes, sir, I made a point of making myself known to the crews going out and coming back.'

Mr Huber seemed impressed because Calum's predecessor had simply not bothered. He was also pleased that the oil production over the past six weeks had been steady. He told Calum that he deserved a rest and that his fiancée could take the rest of the day off as he was going out to play nine holes of golf.

Calum was delighted and he and Traudel left the building and clilmbed into the Lincoln. Virgil ran them back to Traudel's apartment. They undressed and showered together, lathering each other's bodies before heading for the bedroom where they made passionate love.

Later Calum helped his fiancée to prepare the evening meal, and once they had dined, they retired to the bedroom for more lovemaking before they fell asleep.

The following day was a Saturday. It was a beautiful morning with not a cloud in the sky. Calum asked Traudel whether she had used her VW Beetle during the time he was away and she told him that it had not moved since he had gone to Baku.

Calum went out to the car park and tried the ignition. The engine turned over about three times and then fired up. He went back into Traudel's apartment and told her that he was going to telephone his parents in Sussex and update them about his trip to Azerbaijan.

During the conversation they thanked him for his last letter, which he had posted some three weeks earlier.

Later that morning the pair of them motored to Corpus Christi on the Gulf of Mexico and stayed overnight in a motel. They returned to Houston the following day and visited Traudel's parents at their apartment. Traudel's mother Ingrid gave Calum a big hug whilst Horst shook his hand and congratulated him on becoming engaged to his daughter.

Horst produced the Macallan whisky bottle and again filled four glasses.

Calum said to Horst, 'What was it like living in Nazi Germany under Hitler?'

Horst replied, 'I cannot remember the war years because I was born in 1943. But I can remember after the war the total devastation caused by allied bombing. Dortmund had practically been flattened.'

'Did any of your family fight in the war?' Calum asked.

Horst replied, 'Yes, my father had been working in a Dortmund bank when he was conscripted into the Officer Corps and was later attached to the fourth Panzer Army and fought in Russia.'

'Was he always in Russia?'

Horst replied, 'No, he was with the German army when it invaded Holland and he was based in Rotterdam and

The Hague. After he left Holland in 1942 he went to Russia. He never went to Stalingrad. He was in Rostov in the Don region from July 1942 till February 1943. He was back in Kharkov for about three months before going to Kursk, where a huge tank battle took place.' Horst took a swig of whisky. 'His name was Major Otto Fromm; he was a staff officer to a major-general but I cannot remember his name. My father told me when I was a boy that this major-general was shot dead by a sniper's bullet somewhere between Rostov and Kharkov and that the major-general had been buried in Kharkov.

'My father told me he was lucky to survive as he'd been sitting next to the major-general in the back seat of a Horch staff car when the man had been killed. After the defeat of the Panzers at Kursk, the Germans fought a rearguard action all the way back to the Fatherland. My father returned to Dortmund in May 1945 and found that the city was occupied by British troops. He was taken to a camp and interned. He was still in his major's uniform but had never been a member of the Nazi party.

'The manager of the bank where he worked before the war came to the camp and told senior British officers that my father had worked for the bank and had been forced into the Wehrmacht. He was released shortly afterwards but had to convalesce as he had lost so much weight.

'Once fit he went back to work and eventually became the bank manager. He retired when he was sixty-five.'

'Is he still alive?' asked Calum.

Horst replied. 'Yes, he is ninety-three and is still fit and healthy, living in Dortmund.' He picked up the family photograph, which Calum had seen earlier, and Horst pointed at his father.

Calum said, 'So you decided to emigrate to the States?'

'Yes, my cousin had decided to emigrate from Dortmund in 1961 and had ended up in Dallas. He managed to get a job with an aero-engine company. He wrote back home saying how much better the standard of living was and that he had managed to buy an automobile in just six months. That swung it for me and that's why I decided to join him in the States at the age of twenty, though I didn't have two deutsche marks to rub together. That was the year President Kennedy was assassinated, in Dallas, shortly after I arrived,' he added sadly.

'I managed to get a job in the same factory as my cousin and started to save money. I eventually met Ingrid here and soon we were married and later came Traudel.'

Calum sat back and said, 'What an amazing story.'

A short time later Traudel and Calum left the apartment and got into a taxi, which Horst had ordered over the phone. They went back to Traudel's apartment and went to bed.

Mr Huber gave Traudel two weeks off so that the lovers could be together. They spent the whole time in each other's company and drove to different parts of Texas, staying in motels.

After the two weeks were up Calum kissed his fiancée at the airport and flew back to Baku.

Part 3

8

Calum was sitting in his office when his mobile phone rang. It was an oil-rig supervisor who had a serious problem.

He informed Calum that the diamond-tipped drill bit that they were operating had started to wear out and that they would need a replacement within seventy-two hours. The supervisor said that if they could not get a replacement they would be compelled to shut down the rig.

Calum told him that he would get the problem sorted out and that he would ring him back as soon as he got an answer from Houston.

About two hours later, after Calum sent an e-mail to Houston, a reply came back saying that the drill bit could be obtained from Nerovski Oil Tools in Kharkov, Ukraine and to make arrangements to have the piece flown down to Baku Airport and then transported to a supply vessel at Baku docks.

Calum phoned the oil tool company in Kharkov and spoke to the stores manager who confirmed that the drill bit was in stock. Calum asked the stores manager to have it put on an aircraft as soon as possible and flown down to Baku as it was urgently required. The stores manager then dropped a bombshell. He told Calum that to fly it down was impossible as a national strike had started that very day.

Calum said, 'Can you not send it down by rail?'

The stores manager replied, 'I am sorry but the trains are on strike as well. Nothing is moving. This situation has been building for months as wages have not been paid and now there is a showdown with all the governments in the CIS.'

Calum said, 'It is imperative that the drill is brought to Baku as soon as possible otherwise an oil rig may have to shut down.'

The stores manager replied, 'The only thing you can do, sir, is to travel to Kharkov by vehicle.'

'The only vehicle I can use is a Lada Riva – will the drill bit fit into the boot?'

'I think it probably would, but it is no light weight. It would be about two hundred and twenty kilos.'

Calum said, 'Do you know the distance from Baku to Kharkov?'

After a few seconds the stores manager said, 'Approximately sixteen hundred kilometres.'

Calum said, 'OK, I am going to leave Baku right now. I have no idea when I am going to reach Kharkov but I will keep in contact by mobile phone.'

'Have a safe journey, sir.'

After he replaced the handset, Calum shouted downstairs, 'Natasha.'

Natasha came running up because it was the first time she had ever heard Calum shout. She entered the office with a flushed face.

Calum said, 'Sit down, Natasha and don't look so worried. I am not going to eat you. We have a big problem. Did you know that there is an air and train strike?'

'Yes, Mr Breffit, it came over the radio a short time ago.'

Calum told her that he was having to go by car to Kharkov in order to get the diamond-tipped drill bit and that he would take the office Lada Riva.

He sent an e-mail to Mr Huber at Houston telling him about the problem and that he was being forced to travel a thousand miles by car to Kharkov and would contact him when he returned. He also spoke to the rig supervisor and updated him about the strikes. The rig supervisor told him that he would try and slow down the drilling process in order to make the drill bit last longer.

Calum collected the keys from the lower office and set off in the Lada.

He called at his apartment and put a change of clothing into a holdall and collected his Crombie overcoat. He stopped at a bank on his way out of Baku and withdrew a quantity of Ukrainian hryvnia and Russian roubles. He had a quantity of Azerbaijani manats and twelve one hundred dollar bills.

He stopped at a filling station and filled the Lada to the brim with petrol. He then headed off in the direction of Rostov. He found the 1300cc Lada under-powered but he was able to maintain a steady seventy miles per hour.

He reached Rostov after nine solid hours of driving. He was very tired and decided to book into a hotel just before midnight and slept for five hours.

He only had a cup of coffee from the night porter before he took his leave at 5.30 a.m. and reckoned that he had just under five hundred miles to travel before he reached Kharkov. He felt rotten as it was freezing and very snowy.

He stopped at an all-night filling station and filled up, paying his bill in Russian roubles.

He kept the Lada at a steady seventy and the car seemed quite happy. Once he got out on the open road he found that it was deserted. He was on his own.

At about nine he stopped and urinated in a layby. The temperature that morning was well below freezing and he shivered as he stood beside the car. He opened the rear door of the Lada and donned his overcoat and the warmth soon returned to his body. He got back into the car and telephoned Natasha and informed her that he was on the main Rostov to Kharkov highway and he hoped to pick up the drill bit by mid-afternoon.

He drove for another two hours when tiredness started to overcome him. He knew that if he did not stop and pull over he would fall asleep at the wheel. So he pulled into a layby and stopped. He locked all four doors and fell into a deep sleep.

A huge juggernaut passed the stationary Lada and the backdraught made it sway from side to side. Calum stirred and opened his eyes. He had been out cold for an hour and a half. He took a bottle of mineral water from the back seat and saw that ice had started to form near the bottle neck. He took a swig from it.

He pulled his Crombie from the back seat and put it on. He felt like death. He got out of the car and urinated beside it. The cold really woke him up. He walked round the car several times and then got back in behind the wheel. He was pretty sure that he was running a temperature.

He turned the ignition key and the Lada fired up. He selected first gear and moved off.

He drove for about fifteen minutes with the heater at full blast and had to stop and remove his overcoat as he had started to sweat.

He drove west at a steady seventy and at 2 p.m. he saw a sign that read 'Kharkov 80 km'. He quickly worked out that he was just fifty miles from his destination.

He felt like pulling in at the side of the road for another sleep but he decided to keep going. He reached the outskirts of Kharkov in forty-five minutes and saw that he was approaching a huge city.

He stopped on the outskirts and looked at his watch. It was 2.25 p.m. He removed his mobile phone from his briefcase and telephoned the oil tool company. He got through and asked to be transferred to the stores manager.

Calum was given directions and managed to find the company without much trouble. He went into the receptionist's office and she told him that he was expected.

A short time later the stores manager appeared and took Calum straight to the canteen where he was offered a meal.

Calum refused, saying that he was not hungry. The stores manager gave him coffee and then asked him whether he had got chilled.

Calum told him he had fallen asleep in the car and had woken up frozen.

The stores manager went away and returned with a bottle of aspirin and gave Calum two and a glass of water. He told him to keep the aspirin just in case he needed them.

Calum had two further cups of hot coffee and then got up. He looked at his watch: it was 3.30 p.m. Calum told the stores manager that he wanted to get away as soon as possible as the drill was required urgently.

The stores manager asked him why he had not come two-handed and Calum told him that looking back he wished he had taken a second driver as he would have been able to sleep on the back seat.

Calum took the Lada to the rear of the building and parked up. He got out and opened the boot lid. A forklift truck came out through the rear exit with the drill bit suspended. The forklift driver gently lowered it into the boot of the Lada. Two workmen steadied the drill bit as it touched the well of the boot. They manoeuvred it into position and hammered in two wooden wedges so that the bit would not move around in the boot on the journey back to Azerbaijan.

Calum closed the boot lid and saw that the Lada was well down at the rear. This worried him slightly as the mudflaps were nearly touching the ground. He reckoned that the drill bit was nearer to four hundredweight.

He went back into the oil tool company and signed some papers. He received two copies. The stores manager told him where to get some fuel before going back on to the main Kharkov to Rostov highway.

Calum fuelled up the Lada and paid his bill in Ukrainian hryvnia. He then rang his office on his mobile and spoke to Natasha and told her that he had collected the drill bit and that he was now on his way back. Natasha told him that she would contact the oil rig supervisor and update him.

Calum set off in the direction of Rostov. He found it hard going as he was tired but the aspirin had made a difference as he did not feel quite so shivery as he had before leaving Kharkov. He also found that the Lada was struggling on the hills because of the heavy weight in the boot and sometimes he was being forced to go down into third gear to get up the steep ones. When it started to get dark, he switched on his headlights and oncoming traffic flashed theirs at him because his beam was too high.

He pulled into a layby and made the necessary adjustments before setting off again.

He had been travelling for some hours when suddenly the Lada started to misfire. He immediately looked at the temperature gauge and saw that it had crept into the red. It was pitch black outside and it had started to snow heavily. He pulled his Crombie from the back seat and put it on. He got out of the car. It was so dark. He removed the ignition key and walked round to the boot.

The boot light came on and he found the Lada toolkit and the inspection lamp. He opened the Lada bonnet and undid the cap on the header tank next to the radiator and saw that there had been a severe water loss. He put his hands on the top of his head and said, 'Oh bugger!'

He noticed that the windscreen water bottle contained about a litre of fluid. He removed it from the channel on the bulkhead, pulling out two neoprene tubes. He opened the container and gathered up some snow from the ground and squeezed it into the container, into which he then urinated.

His warm urine started to melt the snow. He now had about two litres of fluid in the windscreen-washer bottle. He poured the fluid into the header tank and saw it rise to the minimum mark. He filled the washer bottle with more snow and refitted it into the two grooves on the bulkhead. He topped the header tank up with mineral water.

It was snowing much more heavily now. Calum got back in the car and turned the ignition key and the engine fired up. He knew that the cylinder head gasket had blown and he knew that he did not stand a cat in hell's chance of making it back to Baku with the car in this condition.

He set off and kept his speed down to forty miles per hour and had been travelling for nearly half an hour when he saw the temperature rise up to the red mark. He pulled into the side of the road and stopped. He got out and lifted the bonnet and removed the plastic windscreen bottle. The snow had melted with the heat of the engine. He removed the bottle and poured the fluid into the header tank and again topped that up with mineral water.

He again filled the washer bottle with snow, got back into the car and set off. This time he reduced the speed even more and kept the car at just above thirty.

He drove for another half an hour and again noticed the temperature gauge start to rise towards the red mark. He pulled in at the side of the road next to a sign which read, 'Thorez 20 km'. He thought that if he could make Thorez he might find a hotel and have the car repaired in the morning. He again filled the header tank with melted snow and mineral water and set off.

He had travelled less than half a mile when the engine went off a cylinder.

'Oh Jesus, this is all I bloody well need!' he exclaimed. He pulled in at the side of the road. He opened the glove compartment and removed a packet of Marlboro cigarettes, which Natasha had left there by mistake. He stuck one in his mouth and lit it with the car's cigarette lighter. His first smoke in years. He inhaled and became slightly light-headed. He smoked it right down to the stub and lit another one. He was thinking of his next move. He wasn't sure what to do. He knew that if he stayed in the car overnight there was a chance that he could freeze to death. This was the second time in his life that he was really scared.

He was contemplating phoning Natasha at her apartment to see if she could contact someone in Thorez to come out with a breakdown truck as he reckoned that he was only fourteen miles from that town. He checked his pockets in his Crombie and then remembered that he had put his diary in his holdall, which was in the boot next to the drill bit.

He got out of the car and to his amazement found that it had stopped snowing. He could see the stars in the sky. He noticed a powerful light slightly to the north and reckoned that it was about one or two miles distant. He got back into the Lada and decided to head in the direction of the light.

He drove for about half a mile and then turned north on to a heavily rutted farm road. The road started to get rather steep and Calum was forced to go down to second gear. At one stage he went into first as he had lost so much power. The Lada started to bang through its exhaust. The road levelled out and he was able to go up the gears. He eventually pulled up outside a large wooden farmhouse and it was then that he noticed the powerful security light that he had seen from the road.

He was just about to get out of the Lada when he saw the front door of the farmhouse open and a man standing there with a shotgun pointing at him. Standing next to him was a large borzoi dog, wagging its tail.

Calum introduced himself and told the farmer that he

72

had blown the cylinder head gasket and that the car had gone off a cylinder.

The farmer told Calum to get back into the car and start up the engine.

Calum did as he was told.

The farmer walked over to the Lada and said, 'Switch off your engine. Your engine is running on three cylinders.'

He invited Calum into the farmhouse and he gladly accepted. The farmer removed two cartridges from his shotgun and left the gun standing just inside the front door.

Calum asked the farmer if he could stay the night. He said that he did not want to sleep in the car as he had nowhere else to go.

The farmer said fine.

Calum took a one hundred dollar bill from his pocket and handed it to the farmer. At first he wouldn't accept it but Calum insisted.

The farmer said, 'Do you think the cylinder-head has blown?'

Calum replied, 'Yes, it's blown all right.'

The farmer said, 'Is your Lada a thirteen hundred? Because if it is you are in luck because I have the same car and I have a spare cylinder-head gasket set.'

Calum replied, 'Yes, it is a thirteen hundred. I can repair the engine myself but I'm much too tired to do it just now; I'll do it in the morning.'

They both left the farmhouse and walked over to a shed, which the farmer opened. Inside was a white Lada Riva. The farmer reached for a cylinder-head gasket set from a shelf and handed ito Calum.

'Brilliant,' said Calum.

The farmer stuck out his hand and said, 'I am Feodor Zitov.'

Calum replied, 'Calum Breffit,' taking the farmer's hand.

As they walked back to the farmhouse Feodor saw that

the Lada was well down at the rear. 'What have you got in the boot?' he said. 'The Tsar's crown jewels?'

Calum laughed and opened the boot lid. 'No it's not the Tsar's crown jewels, it's a diamond-tipped drill bit but you were not that far out.'

Feodor laughed. 'Where are you heading for?'

Calum replied, 'I am going to Baku in Azerbaijan.'

Feodor replied, 'You still have one hell of a journey in front of you.' He invited Calum into the farmhouse to meet his family.

In the kitchen were sat three women next to a large wood-burning stove. One was an old lady with a shawl round her shoulders; she had pure white hair and a very wrinkled face. Calum reckoned that she was nearer ninety years than eighty. The second was a woman in her sixties whose hair was beginning to turn grey. The third was much younger, dark haired and very attractive.

Feodor said, 'Please let me introduce you to my mother Lyudmilla. Mother, this is Mr Calum Breffit.'

The old lady did not get up from her chair but just nodded.

Feodor then introduced Calum to his wife, Tatyana. She was small and dumpy with a lot of gold fillings in her teeth. And finally his daughter, Marina, who got up from her seat. She was much taller than her mother. She smiled a beautiful smile and said in a soft voice, 'I am pleased to meet you, sir.'

Feodor turned to his wife and told her to prepare the spare bedroom as Calum would be staying the night. He handed Tatyana the hundred US dollar bill.

Tatyana looked at Calum and smiled and then left the room. Calum could hear her going upstairs.

Feodor asked Calum when he had last eaten and Calum told him that he'd had two cups of coffee when he was in Kharkov.

Feodor told Marina to prepare a meal for the guest and Marina disappeared towards the stove which had a large saucepan sitting on it. After about ten minutes Marina came across to Calum carrying a tray, which contained a bowl of stew. Beside the stew was a quarter of a loaf of bread, which was full of wheat grain. Calum was hungry and quickly devoured the food. He kept dipping pieces of bread into the stew in order to soak up the gravy.

After his meal Calum could feel the strength coming back into his body. He felt so much better and the shivers had completely subsided.

Calum thanked Marina for the meal. She didn't say anything but just smiled.

Feodor got up and fetched a bottle, which did not have a label. Calum saw that it contained a clear liquid. Feodor took out two glasses and filled them up. He handed one to Calum and then knocked the liquid back in one go.

Calum looked at his glass; it must be very strong, he thought, noticing how the alcohol clung to the side of the glass like beads of sweat.

Calum took a sip and held his throat.

Feodor laughed. 'That is vodka made here on the farm. It is more pure than the stuff you buy in the shops.'

Calum heard Tatyana descending the stairs. She entered the room and told Calum that his room was ready if he would like to bring his things in from the car.

Calum got up and walked outside and opened the rear door and removed his holdall. He also removed his Crombie and went back into the house.

Tatanya asked him to follow her upstairs. She walked up and entered a small bedroom. It was a bit austere with no carpet, just a wooden floor with a Persian rug. There was a single bed, a chair and a bedside table with a lamp. Tatanya told him that she had put two hot water bottles into the bed to warm it up. Calum thanked her. He put

75

his holdall on the bed along with his Crombie and followed Tatyana downstairs.

Feodor had already filled the two glasses up with more vodka and nodded towards Calum's glass.

Calum thanked him and consumed the alcohol. After the second glass Calum suddenly found himself becoming very drowsy. He looked at his watch and saw that it was just after eleven.

Feodor saw that he was getting tired and suggested that he retire upstairs. Calum nodded in agreement. He got up from his seat. Tatyana said, 'Mr Breffit, please be careful with the hot water bottles as they are stone and could burn your feet.'

Calum was just about to climb the stairs when Feodor asked him what time he wanted to rise.

'Would five be too early?' he asked.

Feodor smiled and told him that he would rouse him at five.

Calum went upstairs, undressed and got into bed. He shut his eyes and the next thing he knew Feodor was shaking him. Calum stirred and asked him what time it was and Feodor told him it was 5 a.m.

'I have never slept so soundly,' Calum said.

Feodor said, 'When you are ready come downstairs and have some breakfast before repairing the Lada.'

Calum swung his legs out over the bed and scratched his head. He went into the bathroom and ran the hot water tap. It did not take long for the hot water to come through. It was boiling. Calum washed and shaved as he had a pronounced five o'clock shadow.

He came downstairs and saw that on the table was a loaf, butter and jam. There was also a pot of coffee. Both men had their breakfast and when they were finished Feodor handed Calum a large sheepskin jacket as he did not want him to wear his good overcoat when he was repairing the car. Calum donned the jacket, which had cow dung on the sleeves, and followed Feodor out of the front door.

Feodor told Calum to bring the Lada to the front of a large barn, which had its front door closed. It had been snowing heavily and the Lada had about four inches of snow on its roof.

Calum got into the Lada and turned the ignition key. The engine started to turn over but it was reluctant to fire up. Calum tried a second time and it caught. He revved the engine and heard that it was definitely running on three cylinders. He turned round and saw that Feodor had opened a large sliding door and had switched on the lights inside the barn. He had also switched on a paraffin space heater. Feodor beckoned to Calum to drive the Lada into the barn.

Feodor said, 'She's on three cylinders.'

Calum nodded in agreement. He asked Feodor whether he had a tool kit and told him that he could repair the Lada himself.

Feodor asked, 'Are you a mechanic?'

Calum replied, 'Yes. I was a mechanic, but a long time ago.'

Feodor seemed impressed.

Calum worked quickly and methodically and while he did so Feodor stood back and admired his handiwork. He had never in his life seen a mechanic work so fast on an engine. He picked up the dead gasket and said, 'It's a good job you stopped when you did.'

'Don't I know it,' Calum replied.

'Where did you learn your trade?

'I was a Rolls-Royce mechanic in the UK.'

Feodor was convinced that Calum was Russian and was astounded to learn that he carried a British passport.

Calum told him his life history as he worked and Feodor listened intently.

Calum replaced the cylinder-head and torqued it down to the correct settings. It did not take him long to reassemble the engine and in next to no time Calum was back in the Lada, firing it up. She ran on all four cylinders. He got out of the car and undid the pressure cap on the header tank and looked in. There was a circulation and no bubbles.

'Everything all right?' asked Feodor.

'Fine,' said Calum.

Calum was about to get back into the Lada when he noticed a huge engine sitting on two wooden railway sleepers. It had a long driveshaft attached to the front pulley. Calum asked Feodor what the engine was used for and Feodor told him that it used to power a hammer mill and a corn bruiser in the barn next door.

Calum walked over to the engine and saw that the top of it was covered with hessian sacks. He lifted the sacks away and looked down at the massive six-cylinder engine, which had the word HORCH written across the top of the rocker cover. He then spotted a plate at the side of the engine, which read, 'August Horch, Zwickau, Deutschland'.

'Is this a German engine?' asked Calum

'Yes it is. The car is next door. Come, I will show it to you.'

Calum followed Feodor through a small connecting door into another large barn, which contained two tractors and a combine harvester. He then spotted the shape of a large motor car parked in a corner and covered with a large tarpaulin, which in turn was covered in about three inches of dust and corn ears.

Feodor pulled up the front of the tarpaulin and the first thing that Calum noticed was the letters WH followed by two lots of three digits.

Feodor then pulled the tarpaulin further back and Calum noticed the two swastika pennants above each front wing.

Calum felt a shiver going down his spine. Just for a split second he felt that he was in a time warp.

Feodor then pulled the tarpaulin right back to reveal a huge motor car.

Calum started to sneeze and was forced back away from the dust and stour until it had settled. He walked to the front of the car and saw a large letter H on the front chromium grill along with four interlocking rings like a modern-day Audi.

He walked round the car and knew by now that he was looking at a German army staff car. He examined the body and found it to be in good condition with just a few rust spots. He noticed that the 'V' windscreen in front of the steering wheel was missing. He looked inside the car and saw that the odometer was registering just thirty-nine thousand kilometres. There were dark stains on the rear carpet and also on the rear seat, which was made of leather. Calum also spotted dark blotches under the driver's seat. All four tyres were perished and flat but he was amazed to find that both the spare wheels, situated on the two front wings, still contained air.

The car was a cabriolet and the black canvas hood was in exceptional condition because it had been dry stored. Calum ran his finger along the bumper, removing the dust, and the chrome gleamed back at him.

Calum said to Feodor, 'How long has this vehicle been here?'

'Since the beginning of 1943.'

Feodor continued to tell Calum that his father and grandfather had found the Horch lying abandoned near the turn-off to the farm. There'd been nobody around so they'd gone down to the main road in their tractor and pulled it out of the ditch.

Feodor had been a baby at the time. The Horch had been towed back up to the farm and put in the barn where it now was. It had never moved since. Feodor continued to tell Calum that just before Stalin died some time in the early 1950s his father and grandfather had taken the engine out and used it to drive the hammer mill and corn bruiser.

The engine had not been used for about fifty years as the farm got electricity in 1960.

Calum said to Feodor, 'Have you any plans for the staff car?'

Feodor replied, 'No, I don't know what to do with it.'

'Are you prepared to sell it?'

Feodor's eyes lit up.

'Because if you are,' continued Calum, 'I am prepared to give you five thousand US dollars for it.'

Feodor said, 'I sold the car twenty years ago to an old German who paid me five thousand Deutschmarks but never came back for it, and I think by now he would be dead.'

'Well, he has had twenty years to pick up the car and I don't think he will be back now,' said Calum.

'I am so glad that you broke down last night, Mr Breffit. Tatyana will be so happy because we are not rich people. We are hard-working farmers. Come into the house,' said Feodor.

They returned to the farmhouse and Feodor told Tatyana about the deal. Tatyana put her hand to her mouth in disbelief. Feodor then turned to his mother who was sitting by the woodburning stove.

He said, 'Mother, tell Mr Breffit the story about the German staff car that father and grandfather brought back to the farm.'

The old lady looked up at Calum and said, 'It was the beginning of February, 1943. Stalingrad had been saved and the 6th German Army had been captured. I can remember a long column of German vehicles passing at the bottom of our road. The column stretched for several kilometres. I remember the noise that the tanks made with their tracks on the road surface. It was a rumbling noise. There were hundreds of lorries carrying troops. Once the column had passed, my husband and his father drove down to the main road in their tractor and found the German staff car lying in a ditch. They knew that it had been abandoned. The front windscreen had been smashed. My husband looked inside the staff car and saw that there was a lot of fresh blood. He saw the remains of a body on the road surface, which had been run over by the tanks. The railway bridge, which crossed the road, had been destroyed. My husband and his father towed the staff car up here and put it in the rear barn and covered it up. It has been there ever since.'

She then turned and looked at Calum. 'Young man, about twenty years ago, a German man visited our farm. He had another man with him who was acting as his interpreter. The interpreter directed his questions at me. He asked me if I knew the whereabouts of a German Horch staff car, which had been abandoned near the farm in February, 1943. I immediately knew that he was talking about the one in the barn but I became scared in case any of us would get into trouble. I knew the terrible risk that my husband and his father had taken when they brought the car to the farm. Had Comrade Stalin known that we had helped ourselves to a German staff car we would have been put up against a wall and shot. I am deadly serious. We would all have been shot. The vehicle would have been repaired and used by a Soviet general.'

Calum asked the old lady what the German was like. She said that he was about seventy years of age and was very tall and slim with a large moustache similar to Franz Josef. He had been visiting colleagues' graves in Volgograd and was then returning to Kharkov to catch a flight back to Germany.

Tatyana then told Calum that the old German came back the following year and said he knew that the Horch was on our farm. He offered the sum of five thousand Deutschmarks for the car, which was accepted. He worked on the car for about six hours and then left.

'He has never come back,' she said, 'and is probably dead because he would be in his nineties today.'

Tatyana handed Calum a photograph of the German, which she said she had taken when he was not looking. Calum looked at the photograph and got the shock of his life because he was looking at Traudel's grandfather, Major Otto Fromm.

Calum went red in the face and Tatyana asked him if he was all right. He just said he was a bit tired and handed the photograph back.

Calum said that he had to make a call on his mobile phone. The family gazed at the phone because they had never seen one in reality, only on television.

Calum dialled Natasha's number at her apartment, which was answered immediately. He told Natasha that he had broken down near a town called Thorez and was now back on the road to Baku.

Natasha told him that the rig supervisor had been asking about the drill bit. Calum told her to tell him to hold on at all costs and he should have the bit in Baku before midnight. He would be driving straight to Baku docks. He was about to hang up when he said, 'Natasha, is there a supply boat that can take the drill bit out to the rig?'

Natasha replied, 'Yes, Mr Breffit, the *Caspian Belle.*'

Calum wrote down the name and switched off his mobile phone to conserve the battery. He took out his wallet and removed ten one hundred dollar bills and counted them out on the table. He turned to Feodor and said, 'I am giving you one thousand dollars as a deposit for the Horch staff car. When I come back I will pay the remainder, four thousand dollars, or I can pay you the equivalent in roubles.'

Feodor replied, 'Not roubles, Mr Breffit, we prefer dollars.'

Calum now told the family that he had to take his leave as he had a long journey in front of him. The old lady put out her hand, clasped Calum's and held it to her face.

Tatyana kissed Calum on both cheeks as did Marina.

Just then Feodor said that the drill bit would have to come out of the boot and be placed on the footwell in front of the back seat to distribute the weight better. After five minutes Feodor had lifted the drill bit out of the boot with his hydraulic lift on his tractor and placed it inside the car. The car was not nearly so down at the rear.

Calum shook Feodor's hand and got into the Lada. He started it up and was about to engage first gear when Feodor said, 'Mr Breffit, how are you going to move the Horch?'

Calum replied, 'I am going to drive it out of here.'

Feodor replied, 'Drive it! Drive it?'

9

Calum drove down the rutted farm road. He got on to the main Kharkov to Rostov highway and found the Lada so much more responsive after the drill bit had been moved to the rear footwell. Again, he kept his speed to around seventy. He saw that the gritters had been out early and salted the road because it was wet and dark.

He took in fuel at Thorez and again tanked up at Rostov and kept going. He took in more fuel at about five and decided to have a sleep. He slept for an hour and then continued his journey.

He reached the Baku docks at 11.45 p.m. and asked a seaman for the location of the supply vessel *Caspian Belle*.

The seaman pointed at a blue ship, docked at the quay.

Calum parked the Lada next to the *Caspian Belle* and shouted, 'Ahoy!'

A seaman came out of the wheelhouse and Calum explained that he was from Temco International and that he had a diamond-tipped drill bit that was urgently required by one of the oil rigs run by Temco.

The seaman went below and a few minutes later the skipper appeared. He asked Calum if he had the drill bit and Calum told him that it was in the car on the rear footwell and that it was no lightweight. The skipper told him that they would hoist it out of the car. Two seamen climbed up the ladder from the ship and attached a line to the drill bit, which was then hoisted aboard the supply vessel.

Calum took out the papers that he had been given by

the stores manager in Kharkov and asked the skipper to sign the bottom lines. He duly obliged and handed the papers back to Calum.

Calum bade him goodnight and wished him a safe voyage. He got back into the Lada and drove back to his apartment block. It was 12.20 a.m. He put the ignition keys through Natasha's letter box, entered his apartment and poured himself a very large whisky, which he swallowed in one go. He undressed, got into bed and was sound asleep within minutes.

He woke at 9.30 a.m. as he had been too tired to set his alarm clock. He picked up the telephone and called Natasha.

Natasha informed him that she'd got the ignition keys and that the Lada was back at the office. She would pop down and pick him up.

Calum told her that he had had enough of sitting in Lada motor cars to last a lifetime and that he would walk to the office. He would be there in an hour.

When he got to the office he asked Natasha if there were any messages and she told him that Traudel had phoned and that she was worried about him having to travel such a long distance on his own. She also said that an e-mail had arrived from Mr Huber asking Calum to phone him as soon as possible.

Calum asked her about the drill bit and she told him that it had been delivered and had replaced the old one. The oil rig had managed to keep going until the replacement had arrived.

Calum went upstairs to his office and phoned Mr Huber. He reminded him that he had been forced to travel to Kharkov in the office Lada due to air and train strikes. He told him that he had travelled two thousand miles in atrocious weather conditions and that the cylinder head gasket had blown on the return journey and how he had sought refuge in a farmhouse well off the beaten track.

Mr Huber said, 'Calum, you are an asset to the company. Travelling two thousand miles to collect the drill bit was no mean feat. Well done.'

Calum then told Mr Huber about finding the Horch staff car. There was a long silence at the end of the phone.

'Calum, did I just hear you correctly? Did you say just now that you have found a German Horch staff car?'

'Yes, sir. It is lying in a barn on a farm at the back of beyond near a place called Thorez.'

'You have actually seen the car itself?'

'Yes, sir. The car has been stood in the same place since the farmer's father and grandfather towed it off the main Rostov to Kharkov highway in February, 1943.'

Mr Huber said, 'You are not winding me up, son, are you?'

'Honestly, sir, I'm not. I have seen the car, it really does exist. The farmer has agreed to sell me the car for five thousand dollars and I have given him one thousand up front.'

'Five thousand dollars, Calum. That's peanuts. You have stolen it.'

'Well, he seemed happy with the offer,' said Calum.

'Describe the car to me,' said Mr Huber.

'Well, firstly, it is absolutely huge, much bigger than the Silver Dawn. The spare wheels are situated on the front wings and the two Nazi swastikas are on brackets above each of them.'

'The swastikas are still on the car?'

'Yes, sir. When I first saw it I thought I was in a time warp.'

'This is amazing, Calum, tell me more,' said Mr Huber.

'The car has a soft top made of black canvas, which is still in very good condition considering the time it has been stored. There are a few rust spots but that does not present a problem. The four tyres are perished and flat but the spares are still inflated.'

'What about the engine?'

'The engine is out of the car. It is lying on two railway sleepers and was used by the farmers to power a hammer mill and corn bruiser.'

'Is the engine seized?' asked Mr Huber.

'I didn't have time to find out but I do know that it has not turned since around 1960.'

Mr Huber said, 'It will probably be seized after this time. What are you going to do with the car?'

Calum replied, 'I am going to rebuild it.'

'So you really think you could get her running?'

'Oh yes, I think so. If she is completely seized it is possible to unseize her by pouring diesel down the plug holes and leaving her for about three weeks to allow the diesel to seep down the bores. If she is only slightly seized, which is more likely because she has not been exposed to the elements, it would only be a matter of days.'

'How long do you think it would take you to get the Horch back on the road?' asked Mr Huber.

'If I had all the bits to rebuild her, I think it would take me about a hundred hours, maybe a hundred and fifty.'

'Right,' said Mr Huber, 'you have still got another three weeks in Baku. I will send out Igor Mankovich in a fortnight so you can spend the last week working on the Horch. The last time I saw a Horch was in Berlin in the early fifties.'

'I am ever so grateful, sir,' said Calum.

'No problem, Calum, I can't wait to see this motor car.'

Traudel then came on the phone and Calum updated her about the nightmare journey. He told her he would be back in Houston in three weeks.

They spoke for another ten minutes or so and Calum told her about the Horch and that Mr Huber had allowed him his last week of his tour to work on the vehicle.

He left his office and walked downstairs to where the girls were working. He helped himself to a cup of coffee and told them that he would be replaced in a fortnight by Igor Mankovich as he had other things to do. He did not tell them about the Horch in Russia. He simply said that he had to go to Kharkov on business for Mr Huber and that he would be returning to Houston after Kharkov. He said that he would phone the office every day when he was away.

Two weeks later Calum picked up Igor at Baku Airport and drove him to his apartment where he offloaded his luggage. He then drove him to the office where Igor was greeted by the two girls. Calum got the impression that they knew Igor very well.

Calum updated Igor with the problems regarding the diamond-tipped drill bit and told him that should another similar problem arise and there was another transport strike, to go double-handed. Igor agreed with him.

The following day Calum withdrew the four thousand dollars that he was due Feodor. He was delayed half an hour as a bank messenger had to visit another bank to make up the large sum. He also withdrew a quantity of Ukrainian hryvnia and Russian roubles.

Later that day Calum got a flight to Kharkov where he hired a BMW motor car at the airport, paying for it with the gold Amex card. He drove to the Zitovs' farm and arrived at after eleven that evening. Everyone was in bed except Feodor who gave Calum a very warm welcome.

Tatyana and Marina appeared in their dressing-gowns and kissed Calum on both cheeks. Calum counted out the four thousand dollars on the kitchen table and told them that his boss had allowed him the last week of his tour of duty in Baku to work on the Horch.

Tears welled up in Tatyana's eyes. She approached Calum and put her arms round his neck and kissed him firmly on both cheeks. Marina did the same. Feodor gripped Calum's hand strongly. Calum was given a meal and had a couple of vodkas before he retired to his bedroom.

In the morning Calum donned a boiler suit, which had 'Temco International Oil Company' written on the back. He was relying on Feodor's tools to put the Horch together. After breakfast, Feodor told Calum that he had to feed his animals in the byre and that once he had done that he would be able to help him with the Horch.

Calum went into the barn where the Horch engine was standing on the two railway sleepers. Feodor had left his toolkit in the corner so Calum picked it up and placed it next to the engine. He undid the shaft, which was connected to the front pulley that drove the hammer mill and corn bruiser all these years ago. He removed the six spark plugs as it was his intention to try and turn the engine as he did not want to be fighting against its compression.

Calum was looking for a long metal bar so that he could place it against one of the teeth on the ring gear of the flywheel and use it as a lever to see if he could turn the engine. Feodor came into the barn and asked whether he could help. Calum explained what he wanted to do and Feodor went away to look. He came back a few minutes later carrying a long metal pole in one hand and a tyre lever in the other, which had a sharp end. Feodor inserted the tyre lever into the metal pole.

Calum looked at Feodor and said, 'Feodor, you are a genius.'

Calum put the sharp end of the tyre lever between the two teeth and both men then put pressure on the pole, hoping that the engine would turn. But nothing happened: the engine was seized.

Feodor went further back and started to put his full weight on the end of the pole. Suddenly the flywheel moved.

Calum shouted, 'Stop, Feodor, stop.'

'Did it move?' asked Feodor.

'Yes, it moved about one centimetre but we can't afford to move it any further or we could break the piston rings. The bores have probably rusted up. Have you any diesel, Feodor?'

'Diesel? Sure, I have a thousand litres in a tank next door.'

Feodor went into the other barn where the Horch was parked and returned with two large oil cans filled with diesel. He handed them to Calum who poured some down the plug holes on to the top of the pistons.

Calum told Feodor that they would leave the diesel to work its way down the bores and that they would come back in two days and try and turn the engine again. He was quietly optimistic that the diesel would work and unseize the engine. He asked Feodor whether he had a pit and he told him that there was one near to where the Horch was parked.

They went into the barn next door and Feodor pointed to the wooden planks across the cement floor. Calum asked him if he could tow the Horch over the pit and Feodor told him that he could do that easily. He went away and came back with his tractor. He reversed up to the Horch and put a chain round one of the bumper supports. He then attached the chain to a tow hitch on the tractor and told Calum to get behind the steering wheel as someone would have to hold it steady.

Calum opened the driver's door and sat behind the wheel. It smelt musty inside the car. There were a number of cobwebs on the steering wheel and dashboard, not to mention the roof.

Feodor went to the rear of the Horch and pulled the tarpaulin away. The dust from the tarpaulin was horrendous but it did not seem to bother Feodor in the least. He got back into his tractor cab and put it in gear. He moved slightly forward and the chain became taut. He shouted to Calum, 'Is the handbrake off?'

Calum nodded.

Feodor let in his clutch and the Horch started to move forward.

Feodor stopped and got down from his tractor and walked towards Calum. He told him that both rear wheels were locking up.

Calum said that he was not surprised. He got out of the Horch and asked Feodor if he had a trolley jack and a two-kilo hammer.

Feodor went away and a short time later came back hauling a large trolley jack and carrying a large hammer.

Calum took the jack, which he placed under the differential of the Horch. As he was jacking the rear of the car up he noticed the ends of the chassis legs had been cut off and that they had been placed on top of both chassis legs. Calum thought straightaway that there was something fishy about this but he did not mention it to Feodor.

The trolley jack had a ten-ton maximum limit. He began to jack the car slowly and the rear started to rise. Calum reckoned that the car was nearer to two and a half tons than two.

Once he had the car well off the ground he removed the hubcaps and then the wheels with their perished tyres. He took out a wire brush and scraped the surface rust from the brake drums as the last thing he wanted was a fleck of rust entering his eyes.

Once the rust was removed from both rear drums, he smacked them with the hammer. Each time there was a crack and he knew then that the brake shoes were now away from the drums and that the rear wheels should turn freely.

He replaced the wheels and was able to turn them without much effort. Feodor got back into his tractor and the Horch moved freely and after some manouevring they managed to get the Horch positioned over the pit.

Calum got out of the car and removed the bonnet of the Horch, which he placed next to a wall. Feodor came over with an inspection lamp, which he had switched on.

Calum looked at the huge space where the engine used to sit. All he could see was the gearbox with its drive protruding outward. He looked round the engine bay as he tried to work out how best to install the engine.

Suddenly something caught his eye. He moved the inspection lamp nearer the front grill and found a piece of metal that was flat at one end. He moved the lamp nearer to where the object lay on a metal tray where the radiator used to be positioned. He picked it up and placed it in the palm of his hand. He handed it to Feodor who looked at it and smiled at Calum.

'That, my dear friend, is the remains of a bullet,' he said. 'It went through the radiator and struck the front of the engine. That is why it is so flat.'

They both walked through to the other barn where the engine was sitting and looked at the front surface slightly to the right of the fan blade; there they saw a small indentation in the metal.

Feodor pointed with his finger and said, 'That's where the bullet struck.' He handed the bullet to Calum and said, 'A souvenir.'

They both returned to the Horch and removed the brake drums and the huge brake shoes and placed them on the bench. Calum took a small hammer and tapped the end of the brake wheel cylinder but it didn't move. 'Just as I thought,' he said.

'Seized?' asked Feodor.

'Yes, my friend, they are seized solid and they will never operate unless they are drilled out and new inserts put in but I am not going to bugger about with these. I will find replacements somewhere even if I have to go to Germany.'

Calum then chucked the wheel cylinders on to the bench. He replaced the rear wheels and let the car down. He then pulled the jack to the front of the car and jacked it up. As he was doing so he read the front number plate. It read WH-615-618. He then noticed that three-quarters of the front chromium grill had been painted black and that the bottom quarter where the aperture for the starting handle was situated was still chrome. He couldn't see the purpose in painting the grill black. He also noticed that one of the upright spars in the grill had a nick out of it and he guessed that this was where the bullet had first come in contact with the car.

Once the car was jacked up he repeated the procedure with the the front wheels.

That done, Calum asked Feodor if he had a large battery with a positive earth. Feodor went away and came back carrying a large tractor battery.

The original battery had been removed decades past and Calum lifted the new one into the well. He connected the leads and then sat behind the steering wheel. He turned on the ignition key but the ignition light did not come on.

'You prat,' he said to himself. He got out of the car and asked Feodor if he had any insulated wire. Feodor obliged. He asked Calum what the problem was and Calum told him that there was no circuit but he could rig one up with some wire.

Calum made the circuit, got back into the Horch and turned the ignition key. This time the red ignition light on the dashboard came on. He looked for the light switch and turned on the side lights. They came on too.

Feodor was standing at the front of the car and shouted, 'Side lights on.'

Calum pulled the switch out further and the headlights

came on, lighting up the side of the barn. Calum was amazed at just how powerful the lights were.

Over the next few hours Calum carried on working on the Horch, methodically testing, fixing, greasing and lubing while Feodor helped in whichever way he could.

At one point Calum was busy examining the two ends of the chassis legs, which had been cut off. He realised that the ends had at some time been welded back on to the chassis using a brass welding rod and somehow the ends had been cut off again using a grinder. He thought that this was very strange but decided to keep it to himself.

At one o'clock both men went into the farmhouse. Calum cleaned himself up and was given a large bowl of borscht soup for lunch. They all chatted away for about half an hour before Feodor got up saying that he would have to attend to his cattle and would see Calum later. Calum slept in a chair for half an hour and then returned to the Horch.

He put on a pair of rubber gloves and tied a handkerchief over his nose and mouth. He filled an old spray gun with old black engine oil and switched on a nearby compressor. He went under the Horch and completely sprayed the underside. He returned to the Horch engine with the battery and connected them up. He checked the coil and managed to get a spark. He removed the distributor cap and put the blade of his penknife between the contacts and saw that there was a very weak spark. It was so weak that it would never start the engine. He removed the points and cleaned them with a piece of emery paper. He replaced them and found the spark to be much stronger.

He looked at the plugs that he had taken out and noticed that they were long reach; he knew there would not be a problem in finding replacements.

Calum disconnected the battery and put it back into the Horch when he remembered that he had not checked the windscreen wipers and whether the dash panel illuminated. They all worked fine.

He got out of the car and went to the passenger side and took out his penknife and cut round the windscreen rubber.

Just then Feodor appeared. Calum asked him to put his hands on the windscreen on the outside as he was going to push it out. Feodor put the flat of his hands against the windscreen and Calum thumped the inside with the palms of his hands and it came away.

Feodor lifted it away from the car and laid it on some hessian sacking on the bench. Calum told him that he would use the screen as a template in order to replace the other side. He asked Feodor where he could get a new screen and Feodor told him that he would have to go to Kharkov. Calum said that he would go there in the morning and get the job done.

So the next morning he woke early and drove to Kharkov. His first port of call was to Nerovski Oil Tools where he had earlier picked up the diamond-tipped drill bit. He entered the reception and asked to speak to Yuri Lebed, the stores manager.

Yuri appeared within a minute and recognised Calum immediately. He asked Calum about his journey to Baku and Calum told him that it had been a nightmare.

He asked Calum if he had come for another oil tool and Calum explained that he was looking for a firm that could make him a windscreen. He spun him a yarn about having to abandon the Lada with a broken windscreen and having got a lift back to Baku in a lorry and that he was now back to collect the Lada. He never mentioned the Horch.

Yuri picked up a directory and flicked through it. He told Calum that there were three companies that could make or replace windscreens. Two were on the other side of the city but the other one was only two kilometres away.

Calum got directions. He thanked Yuri and left.

He found the premises and went in with the Horch's windscreen and windscreen rubber. He asked one of the assistants if he could make a screen using the old one as a template. The assistant was gone less than five minutes when he returned with the new screen.

Calum asked him where he was likely to get a screen rubber similar to the old one. The assistant said that he had never seen a windscreen rubber like it before. It was not a Ukrainian or Russian rubber, he knew that much.

Calum thanked him for his help and at no time did he mention the Horch. He paid his bill in Ukrainian hryvnias.

He returned to the BMW and wrapped the windscreen glass with hessian sacking to protect it. He drove away from the depot and stopped at a nearby filling station and tanked up.

While he was paying his bill he noticed various types of spark plugs on display including long reach, which would be suitable for the Horch engine. He bought eight just in case he damaged one or two. He got back in the BMW and was heading for the main Kharkov to Rostov highway when he noticed an auto paint shop. He pulled up in front of it and went in.

He asked the shop assistant whether he stocked black cellulose paint, cellulose primer and thinners.

The assistant told him that he stocked all three.

Calum bought five litres of black paint and primer, and ten litres of thinners. He also bought a brand new spray gun and wet-and-dry rubbing down paper, plus a rubbing block and six reels of masking tape. He again paid for his purchases in Ukrainian hryvnias.

He returned to the Zitov farm in the late afternoon and chatted away with the family until they had their evening meal. Calum watched television and went to bed at around ten.

He had been working on the bodywork the next morning for a couple of hours when he stopped to telephone his office in Baku. He was surprised just how good his mobile reception was. He asked Natasha if there were any problems and she informed him that one of the oil rigs was reporting a severe fall in production as the field that they had been working on for the past nine months was drying up.

Natasha said that the mudlogger had taken a core sample about one and a half kilometres north-east of the drying-up field and that Pyotr had gone out on a supply boat and examined the sample under ultraviolet light and it had turned fluorescent.

'Natasha are you sure?' said Calum.

'Yes, it is definite,' she said. 'Pyotr telephoned this morning to confirm it.'

Calum told Natasha to put Igor Mankovich on the phone.

Calum could hear Natasha calling Igor who was upstairs. A few seconds later he was talking to Igor about the favourable core sample and suggesting that he send an e-mail to Houston for permission to move the rig. Calum then asked Igor to check the internet for the telephone number for the Mercedez-Benz museum in Stuttgart.

About twenty minutes later Igor called back with the Stuttgart number.

Calum dialled the number and spoke to a female member of staff. He explained that he was desperately trying to get wheel brake cylinders for a pre-war Horch. The woman at the other end said that she would transfer his call to a colleague who might be able to advise him. A few seconds later a male voice came on the line and asked Calum what he wanted to know about Mercedes-Benz motor cars.

Calum told him that it was not Mercedes he was phoning about but a pre-war Horch.

The German spoke perfect English and informed him that the Horch motor car company had gone out of production either in 1939 or 1940. He asked Calum if he was enquiring about the Horch 853 or the 853A.

'I am not sure,' said Calum, 'it's the Horch staff car that was used by the German army during the Second World War.'

The German told him that the Horch staff car was one of the rarest motor vehicles in the world and that they were utterly priceless. He said that they were only supplied to Hitler's elite. He asked Calum if he had one and Calum told him that he had a friend in the United States who did and was having problems with the braking system.

'What sort of problems?' asked the German.

Calum told him that the wheel brake cylinders were all completely seized as the car had been standing for a long time without being used.

The German asked Calum where the car had been found in Europe and at this stage alarm bells started to ring.

'I don't know the Horch's history and I'm not even sure if it was imported from Europe,' he said.

The German told him that the brake wheel cylinders should not be a problem as they and many other parts used on the Horch and other Auto Union vehicles were the same as those on pre-war Mercedes-Benz cars. In fact, they were still used on Mercedes Fintails up until the 1950s. He asked Calum if he had seen the Horch and Calum said that he had only seen it once.

The two men chatted for a little while longer. The German was a mine of information about Horch and its history and assured Calum that as far as the wheel brake cylinders were concerned he should not have any problems as they were still readily available. He said that there were plenty of good motor factors in Stuttgart that would stock them. He told Calum that if he could hold the line he would give him more information on Horch motor cars.

He was gone for fully two minutes before he came back on the line. He informed Calum that Horch motor cars were built in Zwickau and that the company was known as Firma Horch and that if he wanted any more information about these vehicles he should write to Stadarchiv in Zwickau. He gave him the address and said that he hoped he had been of some assistance.

'Some assistance! My friend, you are a walking encyclopedia. I cannot thank you enough.' Calum switched off his mobile phone and returned to the Horch to begin the rubbing down, priming and painting.

Within half an hour of masking and priming Calum had transformed the Horch from a drab-looking black car into a grey car. Once he had finished he went outside to get some air as the cellulose was beginning to irritate his chest. He cursed himself for not buying a facial mask when he was in the auto paint shop.

He went back in after half an hour and found that the paint had dried. He gave it another coat and decided that two was enough.

10

The following day Calum drove to Kharkov and told the family that he would be gone for a couple of days as he had to get bits for the Horch's braking system. He picked up a mask at the auto paint shop and then drove to Kharkov Airport but could not get a direct flight to Stuttgart.

He had to fly to Tempelhof Airport in Berlin and then get a connecting flight to Stuttgart He arrived and got into a taxi and asked the driver if he knew of any good motor factors in the city. He did.

They arrived at a large motor factor on the outskirts of the city. Calum told the taxi driver to wait as he was returning to the airport. Calum went into the motor factors and explained what he wanted.

The assistant went into the back of the premises and returned with six brand new wheel brake cylinders, which were identical to those he had removed from the Horch.

Calum then asked the assistant if he had any spares for a pre-war Horch.

The assistant told him that he was sure he had some basic spares. He disappeared and soon returned with a cardboard box with various items in it. Calum went through the box and found a brand new coil, contact sets and condensors. Calum bought the lot.

The assistant informed him that if he wanted any more bits for the Horch he should go to the auto jumble in Bremen. He said that it was the largest auto jumble in Germany and that he had been there the previous year and had seen a stall that only sold bits for Horch motor cars.

He said he'd seen a brand new front grill for a Horch staff car and he doubted if the man would ever sell it because staff cars were so rare and that most were in museums.

The assistant's English was poor but Calum could still make him out. He told Calum that the next Bremen jumble was in six weeks' time.

Calum thanked the assistant for his help and went outside to the waiting taxi.

By the time he got back to Kharkov it was late and he did not want to drive the one hundred and eighty miles to the farm as he was too tired. He booked into one of the airport hotels, had a meal and went to bed.

Calum got back to the farm at nine the following morning and immediately donned his boiler suit. He fitted the new wheel brake cylinders and bled the braking system with the help of Feodor. He checked for leaks, and there were none. By the end of the morning the Horch had a perfect braking system. Calum unseized the handbrake and got that working as well.

After lunch, Calum and Feodor went to the Horch's engine and tried to turn it. It turned without much effort. Calum looked at Feodor and smiled. The diesel had worked its way down the bores.

Calum was delighted because he knew that he did not have to strip the engine down, though he would have been prepared to do that if the diesel had not worked.

He found the starting handle in the boot of the Horch and placed in into the front pulley and turned the engine over by hand for about fifteen minutes. It was turning over quietly. He looked at the radiator, which lay against a wall in the barn where it had stood for decades. He cursed himself for not taking it to Kharkov to be re-cored.

That afternoon Feodor reversed his tractor up to the engine and lifted it up by using the hydraulics. He took the engine round to the other barn to where the Horch was standing and gently lowered it in front of the vehicle. Both of them fixed a block and tackle to a beam and then raised the engine. Calum decided that it would be easier to remove the huge front grill of the Horch in order to refit the engine. He did that and then together they raised the engine until it was five feet off the ground.

Feodor attached a rope to the front bumper support and pulled the Horch forward using his tractor until the engine was sitting over the engine bay. By pure luck the gearbox spline went into the rear of the engine first time and the huge engine settled down onto its mountings. The engine was back in for the first time in over sixty years.

Calum punched the air. He shouted, 'Yes!' Feodor smiled and patted Calum on the back. Calum tightened down the huge engine mounting nuts and bolts and those of the gearbox bell housing. He connected up all the wires. He fitted the new contacts, condensor and coil and finally connected up the battery.

He got into the car and turned on the ignition and saw that there was no reading on the petrol tank gauge. He was sure that any petrol would have evaporated over the years and would never start the car.

Feodor went off and came back with two jerrycans full of petrol, which he poured into the tank. During this time Calum had fitted six new long reach spark plugs.

Calum got back into the car and switched on the ignition; the petrol gauge was reading just above the empty mark.

Calum then removed the float chamber on the carburettor and filled it with petrol. He then switched on the ignition and got out of the car. He removed the distributor cap and checked the spark at the points. It was a superb spark.

'Feodor, we have a good spark and we have petrol. This big lady is going to fire up any moment now,' said Calum.

Calum sat back in the car and switched off the ignition. He gave Feodor the thumbs up sign and switched it on again and pressed the starter. The huge six-cylinder engine started to turn over slowly. Calum kept his finger on the button and at the same time moved the choke back and forward.

Suddenly the big Horch started to cough. She was wanting to fire up. She coughed a second time. Calum switched off the ignition and got out of the car. He slackened the distributor drive and retarded it by about a sixteenth of an inch. Feodor asked him what he had done and Calum told him that the engine's timing was too far advanced so he had retarded it. He got back in behind the steering wheel and pressed the starter. The monster Horch burst into life.

Calum revved the engine slightly and knew that it was running on all six cylinders. Feodor was jumping up and down with his hands in the air. He walked up to Calum after he got out of the car, grabbed his hand and shook it vigorously.

'Calum, you are a mechanical genius,' he said. 'I was a teenager when I last heard that engine running. I never thought I would hear it again. You have done enough for today. Let's go inside and celebrate.'

The pair of them went into the farmhouse and Feodor told the women that the Horch engine was running again. Neither of them could believe it. Feodor got out the vodka bottle and before the night was out they had started on a second. By the time Calum got to bed, he was a little bit more than merry. He slept like a log.

Next day Calum telephoned his office in Baku and learned that everything was going fine. Igor told him that Houston had given permission for the oil rig whose production had been falling to resite where the positive core sample had been taken. This was in the process of being done that day.

Calum told Igor to phone Houston and inform Mr Huber

that he had got the engine running and that he had repaired the braking system and that all he needed now to finish the job was to repair the radiator and to find four tyres along with inner tubes. He also told Igor to tell Traudel that he would phone her in the next two days.

Later the same day Calum's phone rang. It was Igor on the line. Igor told him that Mr Huber wanted to know the size of the tyres, so Calum told him. Igor also said that he had spoken to Traudel and that she was missing him dreadfully. They said their farewells and Calum hung up. He noticed that the mobile phone battery was well down so he charged it up that evening.

The next day Calum drove to Kharkov and called at Nerovski Oil Tools where he saw Yuri, the stores manager. He asked him if he knew where he could get a radiator re-cored.

Yuri obviously thought that it was the Lada's radiator that he was talking about and told him that he must have bought a Monday morning car. He asked Calum if he had managed to get the windscreen sorted out and Calum told him that he had. Yuri picked up the directory and found that there were only two firms in Kharkov that re-cored radiators and that both of them were on the west side of the city.

Calum cursed.

Yuri gave him a map of the city and marked their locations.

It took Calum nearly an hour to cross to the west side but he eventually found one of the firms that Yuri had given him.

He took the radiator out of the BMW's boot and went into the building. There was a man behind the counter wearing blue overalls. Calum approached him and placed the radiator on the counter.

Calum said, 'Could you re-core this old radiator?'

The assistant said, 'What has it come off?'

Calum replied, 'It's from an old lorry that my father has on the farm.'

The assistant said, 'Yes, it can be re-cored but not until tomorrow.'

Calum replied, 'I have travelled three hundred kilometres and I don't want to do a double journey.'

The assistant said, 'Wait here,' and went into the back office. After a few minutes he returned and said, 'Because you have come such a long way the radiator will be ready to collect at four this afternoon.'

Calum said, 'Thank you so much. I really appreciate that.'

He got back into the BMW and drove to a nearby restaurant and had a meal. He took a newspaper from a stand in the restaurant and read it from front to back.

At four he picked up the radiator and paid the bill in Ukrainian hryvnia. He placed it in the boot and drove east across the city. He reached the farm at 8.30 p.m. and a meal was waiting for him.

In the morning, Calum fitted the re-cored radiator and Feodor filled it up with antifreeze. He told Calum that the last thing he wanted was for the Horch to be frost damaged after all the work that Calum had put in.

Calum got into the Horch and she started first time. He ran her for about ten minutes and then checked that the antifreeze was circulating in the radiator. It was.

'All we need now is a set of new tyres and we'll have the old lady back on the road,' said Calum.

'Calum, when you said you were going to buy the Horch and drive it out of here, I honestly thought you were mad but you have proved me wrong,' said Feodor. 'You are the best mechanic I have ever met in my life.'

That afternoon Calum sprayed the Horch black. He was able to give her a second coat a few hours later and was pleased that there were no runs. This time he wore the mask that he had purchased in Kharkov and his chest was clear after the spraying.

Just as he was leaving the barn his mobile phone rang. It was Igor Mankovich.

Igor told him that Mr Huber had got the tyres and as one of Temco's oil tankers was leaving the next day from Galvaston en route to Batumi in Georgia to pick up oil he could collect the tyres at Batumi in ten days' time. Mr Huber had bought him six tyres in all: four for the car and two for the spares in the wings. Calum was over the moon.

Calum rose early the next day and worked for a few more hours on the Horch.

His work done, Calum told the Zitov family that he was going to fly to Baku the next morning but would be back once he'd got hold of the tyres. He also told them that he was going to go to Bremen in Germany in around six weeks' time to get more parts for the Horch.

The following morning Calum phoned Igor in Baku and asked him if he knew anything more about the tyres that Mr Huber had obtained for him. Igor told him that they had been put aboard the *Texas Maiden* at Galvaston as planned and she was on her way to Batumi. He said that the captain of the tanker would phone the Baku office the day before he berthed at Batumi.

Calum told Igor that he would see him back in Baku the following day.

11

Igor was waiting for Calum at the airport when he got off the plane at Baku. They got into the office Lada and drove to the office.

Calum asked Igor what had happened to the oil rig whose production was falling and Igor informed him that Houston had accepted Pyotr's findings and the rig had been moved accordingly. The drillers had struck oil at just under twelve thousand feet and the oilfield was massive.

Calum sat back in his seat and said, 'That's the best news I have heard for a while.'

Calum then went into the top office and telephoned Traudel at her apartment. He told her he was sorry that he had not been able to phone her as he'd been at the back of beyond and hadn't been able to get a reliable signal on his mobile; he hadn't wanted to use the farmer's phone because he thought that would be a bit cheeky. He said that he had been thinking about her every day.

Traudel told him that it felt like an eternity since she had last heard his voice. She told him that she loved him and that Mr Huber had updated her about the progress with the Horch staff car.

Later, Calum caught a flight back to Houston and as usual Virgil Johnson was at the airport to pick him up.

At the office, Calum went straight up to the twelfth floor and saw his fiancée behind her desk. As soon as she saw Calum she was off her seat like a rocket and had her arms round his neck and kissed him hard on the lips.

'Thank God you are back,' she said. 'I have been desperate for you.'

Calum told her that the feeling was mutual and that he could not wait to get her back to the apartment.

Traudel told him that Mr Huber wanted to see him straightaway and she went over to Mr Huber's door, knocked and went in. She beckoned to Calum to follow.

Calum walked in and Mr Huber got up and shook his hand. Calum took out several photos of the Horch from his pocket. The first was as it looked when it was first discovered. The second was at primer stage. Others showed the engine sitting on railway sleepers with the long pole attached to the front pulley. The last photo was taken after Calum had sprayed the Horch black.

Mr Huber was amazed at the transformation. He was really impressed and asked, 'Have you got the Horch running?'

Calum replied, 'Yes, sir, she is running like a Swiss watch. The diesel unseized the six pistons and she was then able to be turned by hand.'

'Calum, you amaze me,' said Mr Huber.

'I had to replace the left side of the V windscreen as it was missing and I had to get the radiator re-cored as a bullet had gone right through the front of the radiator and then struck the front of the engine,' said Calum.

Mr Huber stared at Calum. 'You are not telling me fairy stories, are you, Calum?' he said.

Calum placed the spent bullet on his desk.

Mr Huber picked it up and looked at it. 'Well, I'll be damned,' he said.

Calum told Mr Huber that he had information about the discovery of the Horch by the deceased members of the Zitov family. He told him how the staff car had been found abandoned and that there had been fresh blood in the car. How the partisan's body had been flattened by the tanks after being blown off the bridge while the column moved westwards. He reminded Huber that the car had been stored for nearly seventy years and that the family would have been put to death if the authorities had found out.

Calum then told Mr Huber about the elderly German from Dortmund calling at the farm in 1991, shortly after the break-up of the Soviet Union, enquiring about a German Horch staff car, which had been abandoned near the Zitovs' farm.

'The Zitovs told the German that they did not know what he was talking about and he left.'

Mr Huber could not believe what he was hearing; he was absolutely captivated by the story.

Calum then dropped a bombshell.

'The old German came back to the Zitov farm the following year, in 1992, and said that he knew that the Horch was on the farm and offered the farmers five thousand Deutschmarks, which the Zitovs accepted.

'The old German had a Russian-speaking interpreter with him and, according to the Zitovs, the old German worked on the Horch for around six hours before he left and then never returned. When he was at the farm one of the Zitovs took a sly photo of him when he was not looking. They showed me the photograph and I immediately recognised him as Traudel's grandfather, Otto Fromm.'

Mr Huber was shocked.

'Mr Huber, there is something else I want to tell you. When I went under the car when it was over the pit I found two plates, which turned out to be the ends of both chassis legs. I examined them and there was evidence that they had previously been cut off and then welded back on using a brass welding rod. They were then cut off again because the grinder had sliced through the brass welds. I have attached the ends back on to the chassis using fibreglass matting and resin with a hardener. I have smoothed down

109

the matting and painted it black and nobody would be any the wiser.'

Mr Huber said that there was something not right and the only person who could solve the enigma was Traudel's grandfather and that there was little doubt that the chassis legs had contained something that the old German wanted. And whatever was in there was of value.

'The only way to find out for sure is to take Traudel to see her grandfather in Germany,' said Mr Huber. 'Maybe he will tell her the truth, especially as you have rebuilt the Horch and discovered its secret.'

Calum said, 'I'll break the news gently to her.'

'Good boy,' said Mr Huber.

Calum and Traudel walked back to her apartment, had a shower and got into bed and made love. Later that night Calum told Traudel about her grandfather's involvement with the Horch. She was a little weepy at first as she feared that her grandfather had done something terribly wrong. She asked Calum if her grandfather would go to prison and Calum told her that there was no way the authorities would jail a ninety-three-year-old man.

Traudel said that she would go to Dortmund and try and get the truth from her grandfather.

The fortnight went quickly and before he knew it Calum was back at Baku Airport. He was picked up by Igor who informed him that everything was going fine and that there had been no problems with any of the oil rigs or platforms while he was away. Igor told him that the *Texas Maiden* had docked at Batumi and that the captain had phoned the office two days earlier to say that he had six automobile tyres and tubes to be collected. He said that the tanker would be in Batumi for a minimum of ten days before it returned to the States to discharge its cargo of oil.

Igor drove Calum to the office where he was greeted by the two women. He went upstairs to his office and took out a map. He reckoned that Batumi was about four hundred-odd miles from Baku.

He told Igor that he would take the Lada to Batumi the next day and stay there overnight as there was no way he was going to drive eight hundred plus miles in one go. He said that the two-thousand-mile journey to Kharkov and back had nearly killed him.

Calum left Baku at six the next morning and reached Batumi nine hours later. Some of the roads were rutted and potholed and the mountain passes were very steep with switchbacks.

When he reached Batumi he soon found the docks and saw the *Texas Maiden* at her berth. He went up the gangplank and boarded the ship. He asked a member of the crew where he could find the captain, and the crewman pointed at the wheelhouse.

The captain was sitting there with the chief engineer, drinking bourbon. There was a litre bottle on the table.

Calum introduced himself and told both men that he was from Temco's Baku office and he had come to collect six automobile tyres.

Captain Chuck Mitchell got off his seat and shook Calum's hand as did the chief engineer. Captain Mitchell confirmed that they had the tyres on board and had been expecting him. He asked Calum if he was going straight back and Calum said that he had had a rotten journey and would stay overnight if he could find a hotel.

The captain told him that he would give him a cabin and to save his money. He then picked up the bottle of bourbon and poured about a full gill into a glass, which he handed to Calum. Calum downed the bourbon in one go.

'I needed that!' he said.

111

Both the captain and the chief engineer burst out laughing. The captain poured more bourbon into Calum's glass.

In the morning, Calum loaded the tyres and tubes into the Lada. The captain and chief engineer were still in their bunks when he left at six.

He reached Baku at three o'clock and went straight to the office. He took the tyres and inner tubes out of the Lada and left them in the main office where the two girls were working. He explained to Natasha that he could not risk leaving them in the car in case it was stolen.

He went upstairs and had a quick word with Igor. There were no problems and Calum told him that he was going to fly to Kharkov the next day with the tyres. Igor was quite happy to cover for Calum while he was away.

The six tyres and tubes were stored in the cargo hold of the aircraft and, after landing at Kharkov, Calum had to sign some papers before he could retrieve them. He hired another BMW and left the airport.

He stopped at a garage and purchased twenty litres of semi-synthetic engine oil and ten of gear oil. The oil that was currently in the engine was very low grade and they would need to do an oil change.

He drove back to the Zitovs' farm where he was warmly welcomed. He immediately donned his boiler suit and, with Feodor's help, changed the tyres and inner tubes. They then put all the wheels back on including the two spares.

Calum looked at the car from a distance of about twenty yards. The newly painted wheels and the new tyres had completely transformed the Horch.

'It looks unbelievable,' said Feodor. But then he noticed that there was something bothering Calum.

'What's wrong?' he asked.

'It's the number plates, Feodor. I cannot drive out on the open road with these Wehrmacht plates because I would be pulled by the police and I don't want to end up in the Lubyanka or a gulag for that matter.'

Feodor burst out laughing. He told him that if he used number plates from the Don region there was still a strong possibility that he could be stopped but if he fitted a set of West European plates they could not check them against their computer.

Calum agreed and said that British plates were the answer. He said that he would get a set sent over from England by a friend.

Later that day, after doing the final oil and filter changes, Calum went under the car with the engine still running to check for leaks. There were none. Calum got back into the car and put her into first gear and released the handbrake. He slowly let the clutch out and the big car started to move forward. He drove towards the open door of the barn and stopped. He told Feodor to jump in.

Feodor sat on the passenger seat and they drove out of the barn. The cold wind hit their faces immediately as there was no windscreen. It was freezing. Calum could feel the lobes of his ears begin to tingle with the cold. He put his foot down and the Horch took off. He was amazed at the power that was coming from the big straight-six-cylinder engine, which had been built before the war.

Calum drove round the farm and parked outside the farmhouse. Tatyana and Marina came out and looked at the Horch. Tatyana said, 'I don't believe what I am seeing. It is a miracle. Just a miracle.' She kissed Calum on both cheeks.

Calum and Feodor got back into the Horch and Calum drove it back into the barn. Just as he was about to park it over the pit the exhaust blew, making it roar. Calum cursed and said that he hoped that this was the last of his problems. He told Feodor that he would have to get a complete exhaust system otherwise he would never get the Horch back to England.

Feodor suggested they take the old exhaust system off and take it to Kharkov where someone would be able to copy it.

Calum told him that he would leave it for the time being as he had to go to Germany for some other parts, especially the windscreen rubber, and there was always a chance of picking up an exhaust there.

The next day, Calum returned the hire car to Kharkov Airport and flew back to Baku. He asked Igor if there had been any problems and was told that everything had been running smoothly.

Calum told Igor that he was going to Bremen to a large auto jumble to get bits for the Horch and that he would be leaving the next day. He then phoned Traudel and updated her on what he had been doing.

12

The following day he flew to Moscow and then managed to get a flight to Berlin's Tempelhof Airport. He was again successful in getting a connecting flight to Hamburg where he stayed the night. He booked into a hotel and later had a stroll down the Reeperbahn and saw all the prostitutes and transvestites sitting on chairs behind glass windows offering their services. He visited a couple of bars and later went back to his hotel and slept.

The following morning he flew to Bremen. He got a taxi at the airport and asked the driver if he knew where the big auto jumble was being held. He did and would take him straight there.

The site was a large car park near a sports stadium on the outskirts of the city. There were hundreds and hundreds of stalls, some with awnings and some without. He started to walk round the stalls, looking for the one that sold bits for the Horch motor car. He had been looking for the best part of half an hour when he realised that it could take him hours. There were thousands of people milling around the stalls.

He then spotted a uniformed policeman on duty and asked him if he spoke English. He was in luck and the policeman asked Calum how he could help him.

Calum said that he was looking for a stall that only sold parts for Horch motor cars but he didn't know where to look.

The policeman approached one of the stallholders and spoke to him. There was a short conversation.

The policeman told Calum that the man who had the stall for Horch spares was about one hundred and fifty metres away. He took Calum to the stall and Calum shook his hand and thanked him for his help.

A large man was sitting on a chair smoking a huge cigar. He looked up and saw Calum standing there and asked him if he could be of assistance.

'I hope so,' replied Calum, 'but I don't speak German, only English or Russian.'

The fat man smiled and began to speak to Calum in Russian.

Calum learned from him that his wife was from Estonia and that he had lived in Tallinn for a number of years and picked up the language there.

Calum told him that his mother was also from Tallinn and that he had been brought up there when he was little.

The fat man asked Calum what he wanted and Calum told him that he had a friend who had a Horch staff car and that he needed bits.

'What sort of bits?' he asked.

'A windscreen rubber for the front V screen,' replied Calum. 'Oh and a fan belt and any other things that you might have available.'

The fat man got up from his chair and waddled to the rear of his stall. He came back and placed the windscreen rubber on his counter along with half a dozen fan belts, which looked brand new as they still had their original labels attached to them.

Calum asked him whether he had any windscreen wiper rubbers, spare sidelights, headlamps and tail lights.

The fat man said, 'You had better come in here and have a look for yourself.'

Calum followed the fat man to the rear of his stall and the first thing he spotted was the huge front grill for a Horch staff car. The fat man bent down with difficulty and

116

picked up a box that contained brand new windscreen wipers.

'Any use?' he asked.

'Absolutely.' said Calum. 'How come you've got all these spares?'

The fat man told him that his father had worked for Horch in its factory in Zwickau and after the factory stopped making cars all the spares were literally given away for nothing. His father had kept them in a large shed in Zwickau. 'After my father died, my mother contacted me saying that she was going to get the council to dump the spares. I had just retired at the time and decided to try and sell them myself at the Bremen auto jumble.'

Calum asked him about the front grill and how much he wanted for it.

The fat man scratched his head and said that he would accept a hundred euros for it. Calum went straight into his wallet and paid him.

'How much for all the other stuff?' asked Calum.

'You can have them for nothing.' The fat man found another box and took out two brand new headlamps for the Horch staff car. Then he produced a brand new fog light and spotlight plus new side lights.

He rummaged around in other boxes and found a rear number plate light, which was still in its original wrapping.

The fat man went back to his counter and picked up his chair and brought it to the rear of his stall and sat down. He was puffing and blowing. He sat there for a full minute before he got his breath back.

He asked Calum if he was interested in any of the lights and Calum told him that he was but to give him one price for the lot and not to price them individually.

The fat man scratched his head and said he would take a hundred and fifty euros for the lot.

Calum paid him. 'I don't suppose you have any exhaust systems for the Horch staff car?'

The fat man laughed. He told Calum that he had systems for the 853, the 853A and staff cars. 'I used to bring them here but because I never sold any I gave up; they took up too much room in my van. But I reckon I've got at least six complete Horch exhaust systems, all brand new, that you could have, I don't know, for a hundred euros?'

Calum told him that he only wanted one and would pay him fifty euros for it. The fat man agreed.

'My main problem is transporting all these bits and pieces to my site; it's in the Don region of Russia.'

'Not a problem,' said the fat man. 'I could send them down by train.' He picked up his mobile phone and spoke to his wife and asked her to get the phone number for Bremen railway station. She phoned back a couple of minutes later with the number. The fat man then spoke to the foreman at the railway station and asked him if any trains went to the Don region in Russia. The railwayman told him that there was a train that left Berlin once a week for Rostov.

Calum told the fat man to ask if the train stopped at Thorez. The fat man said it did and Calum said that was where he would pick up the spares. The fat man got a price from the railwayman and it came to one hundred and ten euros. Calum paid the fat man.

The fat man said that he would take the spares to Bremen railway station and have them sent to Berlin and put on the train for Rostov. He gave Calum his business card and Calum saw that his name was Kurt Moessner and that he had a Bremen address. Calum put the card in his wallet and shook hands with Herr Moessner and left the auto jumble. He trusted Kurt because he had seen honesty in his eyes and knew that he would not be let down.

* * *

Calum caught a plane next morning and was in Moscow by the afternoon. He was unable to get a flight to Baku and stayed in Moscow overnight. The following day he flew to Baku and was picked up by Natasha who told him that one of the oil rigs had caught fire and that Igor had gone out in a supply boat. She said that she did not know how bad things were. She drove Calum straight back to the office and Calum immediately telephoned the supervisor on the rig.

Calum asked him for a situation report and was informed that the fire had been extinguished and that it had been caused by a short circuit, which was in the process of being repaired. Calum asked him if anyone had been injured. The supervisor said no but that he had been compelled to shut down production as a precaution, though it would restart later that day.

Calum told him to phone him immediately if there were any other problems. He then phoned Mr Huber and informed him about the fire on the rig and that everything was now under control. He also told Mr Huber that he had managed to get all the spare parts for the Horch in Bremen.

'I have also spoken to Traudel about her grandfather's involvement with the Horch,' he said. 'She is happy to ask him why he had been so interested in the vehicle and why he paid five thousand Deutschmarks to the Zitovs.'

Mr Huber told Calum that he would pay for their return fares from Houston to Dortmund when he was next over.

13

So the following week, Calum and Traudel called on her grandfather, Otto Fromm, at his home in Dortmund.

Calum was amazed how straight and upright he was for a man in his ninety-fourth year. He still wore a monocle and his hair and Franz Josef moustache were pure white.

Traudel told him that she was engaged to Calum and hoped to marry in the not too distant future. She then told Otto that Calum had found the Horch at the Zitovs' farm by pure chance and had since rebuilt it and now had it running.

Otto looked amazed. 'I thought it would have been scrapped years ago,' he said.

Traudel, who was a fluent German speaker, told him that Calum had found that the ends of both chassis legs had been cut off and that they had previously been removed and then welded back on.

The old man put his hands in the air and said, 'OK, I will tell you the truth. Way back, in May 1940, a large haul of gold ingots were looted from the Rotterdam bank and all but forty were sent to Berlin. We took those forty for ourselves – me, a major-general and two colonels – and agreed we would share them after the war was over. Three trips were made by car to the town of Biel near Bern in Switzerland. On each occasion ten ingots were put into a large safety deposit box. In all thirty ingots were deposited but on the fourth and final trip the Swiss were stopping and searching every car entering Switzerland from the German side. I didn't want to chance my luck and drove back to Rotterdam where the ten ingots were hidden in the chassis legs of the Horch. In 1942 I was then posted to Rostov in the Don region of Russia.'

'What happened then?' asked Traudel.

'After the defeat of the sixth Army at Stalingrad we retreated to Kharkov. Both colonels perished at Stalingrad and en-route to Kharkov the major-general, Albert Backhaus, was shot dead. I found his briefcase and in it a solid gold fountain pen among other things. The pen remained in my old major's tunic for decades before I came across it again. When I opened it up to fill it with ink I found a piece of paper inside the stalk of the pen. Written on the paper were two numbers: 2961 and 2962 – two safety deposit boxes in the Swiss bank.'

Otto continued. He told Traudel that he had gone to a remembrance ceremony at the war grave cemetery in Kharkov and had met Klaus Backhaus, the major-general's son. He told him about the gold in the Horch's chassis legs and that there was always a chance that the car could be lying on some farm. He said that after the collapse of the Soviet Union he had visited the Zitovs' farm but they had played ignorant: he knew they were nervous and were hiding something. He had gone back two years later with Klaus Backhaus, who was fluent in Russian, and paid the Zitovs five thousand Deutschmarks, which they accepted. He said that Klaus had cut off the ends of the chassis legs and removed nine ingots of gold but could not get the tenth out as it had moved nearer to the bulkhead of the car and he could not reach it. Otto said that there would still be one ingot in the car. He had given Klaus Backhaus five ingots and had kept four for himself; he still had three ingots and part of the fourth. He had been selling bits as scrap gold to a dealer in Antwerp.

Otto got up and went to his desk and sat down. He got a piece of paper and started to write. He handed the paper to his grandgaughter. Written on it were the two safety deposit box numbers along with the name and address of the Swiss bank in Biel. He said that what he and the others had done in Rotterdam was wrong but there had been a war on. He said that he doubted the authorities would jail a ninety-three-year-old man.

They stayed for two hours and Traudel and her grandfather conversed in German. Every now and then Traudel interpreted for Calum to keep him in the loop.

'What would have happened if you and the others had been found out, that you had taken the gold ingots I mean?' asked Traudel at one point.

'We would have stood on the scaffold at Torgau military prison and it would not have been a quick death but a slow strangulation,' he replied.

Calum and Traudel eventually said their farewells to Otto and flew back to Houston. Calum told Mr Huber what Otto Fromm had told his granddaughter.

Mr Huber said that he knew that something of great value had to have been hidden in the chassis legs and now they knew. He asked Calum what he was going to do next and Calum told him that he would complete the work on the staff car and drive it to England in his spare time.

Calum got in touch with his best friend, Roger Brooks, in Sussex and told him that the Horch was nearing completion and that he would need to get a set of British plates.

Roger told him that he would need to see the vehicle and record the chassis number and engine number on an official form.

Calum said, 'Listen, Roger, I can give you this information over the phone.'

Roger replied, 'Calum, I have to see the vehicle myself and write the chassis number and engine number on the form that I send to the DVLA at Swansea. I am not prepared to take short cuts and end up at HQ getting a bollocking from the Deputy Chief.'

'OK, Roger, you win. Once I am back in Russia I will contact you and make arrangements for you to fly to Kharkov, where I will pick you up. You can get a return flight the next day.'

'That sounds fine, Calum,' agreed Roger.

Calum returned to Baku early as he explained to Traudel that he wanted to get the Horch finished. He eventually arrived at the Zitov farm and was over the moon to find all the spares that he had bought in Bremen lying next to the Horch. Feodor had picked them up at the railway station in Thorez.

Calum spent the next two days on the Horch, fitting most of the spares, including the new front grill and the exhaust system.

Roger flew in the following week and was met by Calum who drove him to the Zitovs' farm where he was introduced to the family. The same day Roger saw the Horch and was absolutely gobsmacked at its beauty and size. He soon found the engine and chassis numbers and wrote them down on the form. He also recorded the numbers in his diary just in case he lost the form.

Tatyana and Marina had made a lovely meal for their guests and that evening they shared a bottle of vodka with Feodor before retiring to Calum's bedroom, which now contained two single beds.

The following day Calum drove Roger back to Kharkov Airport for his flight to London. Calum asked him how long it would take for the Horch to be allocated a British number plate.

Roger told him that it was anybody's guess but not longer than three weeks.

Calum then asked Roger if he had any leave due and Roger told him that he was due ten days and could take them any time.

They agreed that once Roger got the number plates he would fly out on a single ticket to Kharkov at Calum's expense. Once the plates were on the car they would drive it back to England together.

After three weeks, Roger contacted Calum and told him that he had the new logbook and the number plates.

They settled on a date and soon afterwards Calum picked Roger up at Kharkov Airport in Feodor's Lada Riva.

The following morning Calum drove the Horch out of the barn. The Zitov family were all standing outside the farmhouse but the old woman, Lyudmilla, stayed indoors with the big borzoi dog. Tatyana and Marina both wept and Roger went over and gave them each a hug.

Calum got out of the Horch and also embraced the two women. Roger and Calum then shook Feodor's hand and they both noticed tears in his eyes.

Marina said, 'Will we ever see you again, Calum?'

'We will both be back, and don't worry, we will keep in touch,' promised Calum.

Calum said that he was going to drive to Thorez to fill up with fuel before heading off towards Kharkov.

Part 4

14

Calum and Roger got into the Horch and Calum started her up. He engaged first gear and moved off down the rutted farm road and then turned left towards Thorez, which they reached in twenty minutes. They filled the Horch's petrol tank and came back on to the main Rostov to Kharkov highway. As they neared the Zitovs' farm they saw Feodor's Lada parked at the bottom of their farm road. Calum tooted his horn as they passed and the whole family waved in response. Both Calum and Roger had lumps in their throats.

They drove for about eighty miles and then turned west towards Donetsk. After four hours Roger took the wheel. They took in fuel after travelling three hundred miles and it was nightfall when they crossed the border into Moldova. The border guards gave them a cursory glance and waved them through. Roger woke Calum and asked him to take over as he was getting tired; he had driven for five hours while Calum slept.

They crossed the border into Romania and fuelled up again. At the border into Hungary there was no one to be seen. Calum drove for another five hours and woke Roger up as they neared the Austrian border. When they changed over, Calum opened the hamper that Tatyana had given him and helped himself to a sandwich and a cup of coffee. He passed a sandwich over to Roger. Five hours later they reached the Swiss border where they were stopped and had to purchase a windscreen sticker in order to use the Swiss motorways.

Another five hours and they reached the French border where they stopped to stretch their legs. Calum checked over the Horch and found that the oil level was still bang on the mark. He checked the radiator level: also normal.

They crossed France and finally reached Dieppe at 8 p.m. The first thing they did was find a restaurant where they both shaved in the toilet and had a meal. They caught the ferry to Newhaven at eleven and got their heads down and slept all the way.

They arrived in Newhaven just before one and before they knew it their journey was over and they were back in Brighton, parked up about fifty yards from Calum's front door. Once inside, they opened a bottle of wine in celebration and pretty soon after crashed out.

The following morning, they showered and dressed before heading out to a nearby cafe for bacon rolls and coffee. They discussed the ingot that, according to Otto was still in the Horch's chassis leg.

Calum suggested they take take the Horch to his parents' house at Ringmer as there was a pit in their garage.

Roger said that it would be better to go to the local police station in John Street and have the ingot removed there because at the end of the day it would have to be handed over to the police because it was stolen property.

Calum agreed and they drove the Horch to the car park at the rear of the police station.

Once inside, Roger knocked on Superintendent Guy Sheldrick's door. 'Come in,' the superintendent shouted.

Roger and Calum went in.

'And what can I do for you, Roger?' asked Sheldrick.

'It's not me sir, it's my pal, Calum, who will tell you the story from beginning to end.'

Calum took about fifteen minutes to lay out the facts.

Superintendent Sheldrick asked where the Horch was parked and Roger told him.

The superintendent told Calum and Roger to bring the car into the workshop, which had a ramp.

Sheldrick asked Calum which chassis leg contained the ingot and Calum told him that it was the offside and that it was well down near the front.

A mechanic approached with a grinder but Calum told him that it was not necessary as the ends were being held on with fibreglass matting and resin and that a two-pound hammer would easily separate the end from the chassis with a hard tap. The mechanic struck the rear end and the bit came away.

A powerful torch was used to look down the chassis leg and when the superintendent said he could see sackcloth but no ingot, Calum told him that the ingot was wrapped in sackcloth and had been there since 1940.

The superintendent said to the police mechanic, 'How are you going to get that obstacle out?'

The mechanic replied, 'With a long shaft with a metal plate bent to a right angle.'

Calum said, 'Why not try three broom handles tied tightly together, which should be the length of the chassis leg?'

The broomhandles were found in the cleaner's department and the three were tied together. A suitable plate was screwed into the handle shaft. A detective sergeant who had joined them placed the makeshift tool into the chassis and managed to get the right-angled plate over the object. He said that he needed a hand because what he was trying to pull out was very heavy. Calum and Roger lent their weight and half a minute later the ingot was brought to the end of the chassis.

The detective sergeant lifted the ingot out of the chassis, saying, 'What a weight!' The ingot was still covered in sackcloth but when that was removed it gleamed.

Calum and Roger drove the Horch off the ramp and parked it in the car park and went upstairs to Sheldrick's office where they saw the ingot sitting on top of his desk.

He told the pair to take a seat and picked up the phone to ring Scotland Yard. He asked to be put through to the National Central Office for Counterfeit Currency. A short while later he was speaking to Superintendent Mervyn Summers who worked from that office. He told him the story of the ingot.

Mr Summers told him that he had a contact at the Bank of England in the City and he would phone back fairly soon.

After about twenty minutes the phone rang.

Summers told Sheldrick that the ingot should have six numbers stamped on its top edge. It should also have the year of manufacture and its weight in kilograms.

Sheldrick gave him the numbers over the phone and told him that there were apparently thirty others held in two large safety deposit boxes in Biel, Switzerland.

Mervyn Summers said that Sheldrick and the witnesses should come to Scotland Yard as this was now a case for the Serious Crime Squad. 'Oh, and one more thing,' he said, 'it is worth nearly half a million pounds so please don't lose it on your way up to the Yard.'

At the Yard they met Summers who took them to meet the assistant commissioner who wanted to have a word with them. They went up several floors to his office and went in.

Sheldrick removed the ingot from a holdall and placed it on the assistant commissioner's desk. He told him that there were thirty others in two safety deposit boxes in a bank vault in Biel near Bern.

Calum was asked to give his account and took fifteen minutes from beginning to end. The assistant commissioner said that it was a fantastic story and thanked Calum and Roger for recovering the ingot. He said that two senior officers from the Serious Crime Squad would travel to Bern and liaise with the police there. A search warrant would be obtained as the gold in the Biel bank vault was stolen property. He told Guy Sheldrick that he would keep him informed about events in Switzerland.

The mission was a success: the boxes were located and opened and as expected each contained fifteen gold ingots. All thirty were transported to Bern police headquarters and locked away.

Inevitably the story was leaked to the Press who went to town on it. The Dutch Ambassador in Bern even made a formal request for the full four thousand Dutch ingots to be returned to Holland. An emergency meeting was held in the Swiss Parliament and it was decided to allow Swiss police access to bank vaults that had remained closed since the end of the Second World War.

Shortly after this decision, the police in Zurich received an anonymous telephone call from an old railwayman who had worked for the Swiss railways at Zurich railway station. He told them that in January 1945 he had been on duty when a train had arrived at three in the morning. He knew that the train had come from Germany. Several men dressed in civilian clothes had stood next to a number of trucks that were parked on the platform. A forklift truck had been used to lift off wooden crates from the railway carriages and place them on the trucks. One of the crates had fallen off the forklift and on to the platform, splintering the wood and spilling out gold ingots. The ingots had been quickly covered over with a tarpaulin to prevent prying eyes.

The following day, the chief officer in the Bern police received a list of vaults that had remained closed since the end of the war. Copies of the list were sent to city and provincial chiefs of police. The number of vaults involved were never made public.

The police in Zurich entered a large bank where one

131

vault had been opened after nearly seventy years. The only thing that it contained was a stash of four thousand Dutch gold ingots.

After some time, Superintendent Sheldrick called Calum and Roger into his office and updated them on what had happened and thanked them both for their help. Shortly afterwards both Calum and Roger received an invitation from the Mayor of Rotterdam to attend a function in their honour where they were both given the freedom of the city.

Calum loaned the Horch staff car to the National Motor Museum at Beaulieu. It looked fantastic and had the laundered swastika pennants back on both front wings.

Calum returned to the States and married Traudel soon afterwards but he did not give up his Brighton flat as he was a frequent visitor to his native Sussex.

Otto Fromm was seen by police in Dortmund and had to hand back the three gold ingots that he still possessed. No further action was taken against him because of his age. Klaus Backhaus, who lived in Koblenz, vanished off the face of the earth and was never heard of again. He would have been a very rich man.